Identity Theft

It's Murder!

Connie Murray Slocum

First Edition

Oshawa, Ontario

Identity Theft: It's Murder!
by Connie Murray Slocum

Managing Editor:	Kevin Aguanno
Copy Editor:	Susan Andres
Typesetting:	Charles Sin
Cover Design:	Troy O'Brien
eBook Conversion:	Agustina Baid

Published by: Crystal Dreams Publishing
(a division of Multi-Media Publications Inc.)
Box 58043, Rosslynn RPO, Oshawa, Ontario, Canada, L1J 8L6.

http://www.crystaldreamspublishing.com/

Paperback	ISBN-10: 1591463777	ISBN-13: 9781591463771
Adobe PDF ebook	ISBN-10: 1591463785	ISBN-13: 9781591463788
Microsoft LIT ebook	ISBN-10: 1591463807	ISBN-13: 9781591463801
Mobipocket PRC ebook	ISBN-10: 1591463793	ISBN-13: 9781591463795
Palm PDB ebook	ISBN-10: 1591463815	ISBN-13: 9781591463818

Published in Canada. Printed simultaneously in the United States of America and the United Kingdom.

CIP data available from the publisher.

This book is written for, and dedicated to,
Sempai Tina Macaluso of Tiger Schulmann's Karate.

She is a young woman with fists of fury, legs that can level a
two-hundred-pound man, and a heart that's sweet and gentle.

You'll make a fine Sensei one day.

Acknowledgements

With special thanks:

- To my fellow author, Gift Sailor, for helping me with some of the research that finally brought this work to fruition.

- To Matthew Edward Murray, my brother, for talking me through some very rough spots while creating this novel.

- To Cynthia Massaro, my new friend and confidante, whose gentle strength astounds me daily.

- To Kevin Hickey of First Class Photography in Carlstadt, New Jersey, for the jacket photograph.

- To James Slocum, my son and the love of my life, for the photographs in the original text.

- To David Slocum, my husband and the sole owner of my heart for his love and support, as well as the cover shot on the original work.

- To the Senseis of Tiger Schulmann's Karate (you know who you are) for their unwavering belief in me, even when I didn't believe in myself.

Thank you all from the bottom of my heart.

Love,
Connie

It's Murder...

He pulled her from the pillow flat onto her back and climbed on her chest with his knees on each side of her head, her arms pulled tightly above her tearing the taped skin at her wrists, as the headboard moaned in creaking stress. What was he doing? She struggled and squealed from underneath the duct tape blocking the noise.

She had never been more frightened than she was at that moment. Terror gripped her brain, and horror ripped through her mind. He pulled the duct tape off her mouth without mercy and held his hand over it instead. Her mind exploded.

The stinging pain seared through her jaws. Her lip bled from the harsh removal of the tape, and the copper-tin taste of blood on her tongue nauseated her. He reached over, took a little cup off the night table, and put one hand around her neck with his fingers, using her jaw to steady her head. On the night table were baby lotion, powder, and something looking like loose baby wipes too. Reality infiltrated her brain. He was choking her. This was it. She struggled and cried frantically, to no avail.

The cup had brown liquid in it that smelled as if it were an alcoholic beverage of some sort, as it got closer to her face. She didn't want it and tried once again to free herself, squirming and shaking with every ounce of her strength. She moved her head back and forth but it did little to deter the inevitable. His knees held her head in place while his legs brought unbearable aching pain to her biceps. She began to sob from deep in the back of her throat. He held her nose. She tried to move her head away with every ounce of her being. She choked on the liquid, as he poured it into her. She was petrified. She wanted him to stop. She couldn't breathe, and panic swept over her.

"Now, take your medicine like a good little girl," the killer taunted, removing his hand to rub her throat, forcing her to swallow what remained in her mouth.

She tried to scream, but he poured more of the vile liquid into her mouth and held her nose. She tried to move her head back and forth, but his knees held it tightly in place. The liquid found its way into her nostrils, burning as it exited onto her face. Her eyes rolled back painfully into the tops of her sockets, and the world around her imploded. She swallowed, choked, and coughed until he'd gotten about two and a half ounces into her.

The rest was all over her face, but it didn't matter to him. Bathing her would take care of that mess. The date rape drug was in the alcohol. Reality slipped away from her mind's grasp within seconds, and only minutes passed before she was completely out of it, and the killer had total control. He stepped back and took in the scene. This one had been difficult. He considered it his masterpiece.

He untied her, removed the duct tape, and carried her slight body easily to the bathtub. He put her into the water gently, slowly submerging her until she was completely underneath the surface. He stroked her hair lovingly, as she lay still just an inch or two under the surface of the clear water.

He adored how her hair lightened and flowed in the water. He loved that part the best of all. Little bubbles popped to the surface, and he knew that it wouldn't be long before she was dead. It excited him, and he felt his body react to the excitement.

The noise stopped, and everything stood silent and still. White light surrounded her. It was quiet and serene. She floated in the softness of white silk and magnificent warmth. There was no sky, no earth, and no boundaries. It was beautiful; she was beautiful, tranquil. She saw herself through loving eyes. The answers to life came to her, beginning with one time-altering moment—the moment of discovery—and then whirling, spiraling, twirling epiphany...

Pat positioned her camera to get a full-length, tight shot of the body of a young woman that had been murdered. The woman had short black hair, caramel-colored skin, blue eyes, and weighed one hundred pounds at the most. She was lying on her side on her own bed. She had her left thumb in her mouth, as if she were a baby sucking it for comfort. She was completely unclothed, except for a makeshift diaper fashioned from a towel and banana hairclips. There were pillows on each side of her, positioned as if she were a tiny child who might roll off the bed and get hurt. She was recently bathed, powdered, and lotioned, as a loving mother might do to her infant. A chill shot down Pat's spine, causing an involuntary shiver. It was the ninth scene of this type.

The killing spree had come to be known as the Baby Diaper Murders. A serial killer was loose, and no one could connect the victims in any way. They all had different jobs or took different classes at the school or no classes at all. They were from completely different backgrounds. Their hair and eye colors were different. The law officials did not believe that the murders were completely random, even though no pattern in the victims was emerging. Instead, they were sure that a serial killer was behind the crimes because the bodies were left in the same manner. The question was the connection. What were they missing? The answer eluded them, frustrated them, and remained unknown. The norm of serial killers is to kill the same type of person for a reason, wayward as it might be. This killer was not doing that; it was a spree of complete odyssey.

This current victim was eighteen—sweet and reserved, according to her friends questioned at the scene. She was a hairdresser working in the salon just down the street and taking courses at the college to better herself. Her name was Daniella Hernandez.

"Dani was the nicest person. Who would do this?" Pat heard one of the victim's friends say through an evolving sob, as she snapped another photograph.

"Your name was Dani?" She quietly asked the victim, not expecting a response, while positioning the camera to get a closeup of the victim's face. What were those marks on her neck? Had she been strangled or drowned? She took a picture of the marks. Something about them triggered a wave of tension inside her brain. The answer was here.

Pat's mind began churning. Events of the nine murders to date fell into place, as the thoughts spun haphazardly through the space-time continuum in her brain. She knew. She felt it. The answer had been there all along. She lined up the facts, as she knew them, and the story fanned out in her mind, moment by moment, from the first moment she'd found herself involved in it. The answers played out as chapters in a story might.

CHAPTER ONE

P at had packed up the old dilapidated Buick with her
most precious possessions, kissed her parents good-bye,
and headed off to the new life awaiting her. She was
going to college. The old blue beast with its gray, peeling roof
was going to take her there. It was exciting and frightening at
the same time. She would be living on campus and studying
to become an intricate part of solving crimes. In her educated
opinion, forensic science was a brilliant light into making
the world a better place if she was lucky enough to have the
opportunity to join that force. She intended on being the lucky
one, or at least the hardest working one that carried the highest
grade-point average, who would surely be picked for any
position that she applied for.

She read her map carefully because she was picking up
three other potential college students on the way to the school
to help defer the cost of the trip. The Buick, though not the
prettiest of cars, was big enough to carry all four girls and their
new state of compressed lifestyles to the college, or at least she
hoped so.

The old clunker had been good to her parents for the many
years they drove it, and now, Pat was sure that it would do the
same for her. Beauty was in the eyes of the beholder after all,
and if the abominable thing got her from point A to point B
without a hitch, then it was beautiful to her—the ticket to the
life she wanted more than she'd ever wanted anything else.

The first house was only forty-five minutes from hers and
belonged to a girl named Sundance Joy Chyna. She drove

down the street Sundance lived on slowly until she found the number and pulled into the driveway. She wondered what the girl would be like.

It was a small urban neighborhood where all the houses on the block matched. The colors were bright and airy, and the neighborhood seemed well kept. She had found the house she was looking for easily among all the others. The suitcases and bags in front of the house were a dead giveaway. She took a deep anxious breath, hoping that the ride with these complete strangers would not be a huge mistake.

She parked the car and got out. The house was a sweet little two-story ranch, painted white with flowers lining the front and white picket fence surrounding the house. The driveway and walk were made of pink bricks laid in much the same fashion as the proverbial yellow brick road had been in one of her favorite childhood movies, *The Wizard of Oz.*

Pat took in the whole scene, which reminded her of an animated movie or a kid's storybook illustration. She half expected little gingerbread men to come out the front door, dancing and singing merrily. She knocked on the door.

"Door's open," a male voice grunted.

Pat went inside. She felt a little shy about not being escorted in by someone. A man sat in a recliner, as the door opened into a living room. The man was holding a remote control in one hand and a nasty smelling stogie in the other. A gingerbread man, he was definitely not.

"Who are you?" he asked rudely.

His round stomach contracted, as he spoke, lifting his filthy, stained sleeveless T-shirt up to expose the hairiest navel she'd ever seen. Seeing him in the T-shirt gave her a full, unbridled understanding of why that kind of shirt was *affectionately* known as a wife-beater.

He stuck the stogie between yellowing teeth and glared at her through slits containing blue eyes. The stale stench of cigar smoke overwhelmed her, and she fought not to grimace.

"I'm Pat. I'm here to pick up Sundance for college," Pat replied politely, fighting hard not to react to the horrendous smell.

"Sit," he grunted out an order and pointed to a love seat against the wall next to the front door.

"Sunny, you're ride is here," he shouted unceremoniously into the air.

Pat reluctantly moved toward the love seat. Her mind reeled at the thought of the crusty, disgusting man being inside the fairytale house. The fantasy went from gingerbread men singing to old cartoon character cigar-like people flopped over furniture and coughing, wheezing, and gasping for their lives.

Another man came through a small door across from Pat with a flushing sound following him into the room. He planted himself on the seat next to Pat. She unconsciously moved over to avoid contact with the second vile man. He matched the man in the recliner, except that his body odor finalized the ambiance in the room. She shook off the knowing thought that the man had probably not washed his hands, either.

Pat looked around at the room. It didn't match the ambiance or the men. The room was impeccably clean and cheerful. The walls were sunshine yellows, with pictures and memories strewn pleasantly across the room. The furniture was Maplewood, Ethan Allen. It was nice. A country aura seemed to be the theme.

A beautiful, tall woman dressed in high heels and a fifties-style dress came bouncing out of what Pat assumed was the kitchen with a tray of crackers and cheese in her hands. She fit the fairytale look outside the house. She had a short perky style to her brown hair and big brown eyes. She wore red lipstick and pearls and smiled incessantly, as she served the men the crackers. She reminded Pat of June Cleaver from the old Nick at Nite show, *Leave it to Beaver*, except that extra sugar literally dripped off her in excess, where June had more of a personality.

"Hello, dear, I'll get Sunny for you. She's almost ready," the woman sang just before she skipped off to get her daughter.

The surreal foundation of the moment was as noticeable as a train veering off track and making its way through the living room. Pat smirked. She wondered what these people had given birth to.

She half expected this petite little wonder in a dirty sundress with an old smelly cigar stogie hanging from her perfectly painted lips to come prancing out behind her mother, expecting Pat to load her things in the car because she was too delicate. Pat sighed. It would be just her luck.

A few minutes later, that fear was put to rest when Sunny entered the room. Poor Sunny was an exact replica of her father. She couldn't have been less dainty. She had to be more than six feet tall, and she was huge. No cigar hung from her thick lips, and they were unpainted, dry, and cracked. She wore her hair in a buzz cut, and her clothes were manly to say the least, but she was squeaky clean. There was no way she would be skipping or prancing anywhere. Pat was astonished but again fought to maintain control of the emotion and any facial expression that might accompany it. She helped Pat load her things into the car. Then, they walked back in to say good-bye to Sunny's parents before leaving.

"I just need to get my backpack out of my bedroom, and we're all set," Sunny informed Pat in a gentle submissive type of tone. The tone did not fit her physique. Pat took her position next to the creature that was on the love seat to wait.

"Man, she's got some set of ham hocks," the man next to her on the love seat said, shaking his head. He was referring to Sunny.

"Yeah, she's a looker all right," Sunny's father answered in a disgusted voice with rolling exasperated eyes.

Pat was horrified. How could a father talk like that about his child? She didn't like him, and she didn't care if it showed or not. She was flabbergasted at his actions toward his daughter in front of a total stranger, never mind people that were part of her life.

"Now, Ralph, you know she can't help it," Sunny's mother interrupted.

"She could help it a little," Ralph's friend answered shoving an entire cracker into his mouth while the crumbs dropped down the front of him.

Pat listened in stunned silence. It was appalling. Evil thoughts filled her mind. She squashed them, as they reached the tip of her tongue. It wasn't her place. She did not know these people at all.

"Tiffany-Crystal, why didn't you teach her?" Ralph accused.

"Lord knows I've tried. It's to my shame that she looks the way she does," Sunny's mother answered, averting her eyes to the floor.

She had the same submissive tone in her voice as her daughter did. Pat was horrified. What planet was this woman from? Did she not realize that society had changed in the last century? She didn't have to put up with that, neither did her daughter. These men clearly needed a lesson in human tactics and kindness, if not *a mirror*.

"First, you gave me a female. As if that wasn't bad enough, you couldn't train her right?" Ralph continued, gritting his yellow stained teeth, as he spoke through the rancid cigar. His friend nodded in total agreement. He also thought that Tiffany-Crystal had not done her job and that Sunny was living proof of that fact. Tiffany-Crystal took the abuse, as if she were a trapped slave dominated by a master that would beat her, otherwise.

Pat was revolted, but said nothing. She shook her head and tried to gain control of emotions that were on the brink of running amuck, unnoticed by the others in the room with her. How was it that these two grown men did not know about the X and Y chromosomes that made up a child's sex? How was it that they did not know that the male of the human species determines the baby's sex? What century were they living in while the rest of the world had evolved to this one? Next, he would be looking to chop off her head.

Sunny emerged from her room. She seemed unaware of the conversation that had taken place between her parents. Pat felt sorry for her. Looks were not everything, but much too often, they were what the world judged people by.

Sunny said good-bye to her parents. Ralph barely acknowledged her, except he told her to get her fat ass out of his way so that he could see the game on television. Tiffany-Crystal waved merrily, as they drove off. She seemed almost oblivious to what had gone on in her own home. She was the epitome of the "dumb blond" the world identified with in too many jokes to count; either that, or she was just a blithering simpleton, plain and simple. Had that scene actually happened, or had she dreamed it? Sunny didn't seem upset or thrown by the scene. Pat was completely disheveled mentally over it.

They proceeded to pick up the other two girls. The other girls were neighbors and best friends. Their names were Candy and Annie. They had gone to high school together, were cheerleaders together, and had been an inseparable pair since they'd met in the third grade. They were birds of a feather, too, so to speak.

Candy gushed over the many men that had shared her life to date, while Annie continuously looked in the mirror to be sure that the three seconds passed had not ruined her makeup job. Pat exchanged a look or two with Sunny during the conversation with the two other girls. Sunny said nothing, but her eyes said it all. They were in silent agreement. It takes all kinds.

There was a beautiful girl next to a broken down car on the side of the road. A truck full of young men had obviously stopped to help her. Even in the protection of the Buick, Pat could see the men falling all over themselves to flirt with the beautiful girl. She didn't need to hear what they were saying.

"She sure is beautiful," Sunny remarked, pointing to the scene as they drove by.

Pat agreed. She didn't say so, but she wondered if Sunny was wishing that she were beautiful like the stranded girl just then. She was definitely magnificent. Candy and Annie noticed the scene, as Sunny spoke, and they each had a slightly different opinion.

"I don't like anyone prettier than me, not that she is up close. I think that they should all be killed in a humiliating, embarrassing way," Candy said flippantly while fixing her hair in Annie's mirror.

"Maybe we should just mark their faces up for life," Annie agreed.

"Well, killing them would be better. I bet she has bad skin when you get closer. Good riddance to the facially impaired," Candy continued her train of thought.

"What about me? My skin is awesome," Annie said in protest, knowing that she was very pretty and that everyone else thought so too. Candy thought for a moment, while she reapplied her lipstick for the umpteenth time.

"Well, I can take you because you're as pretty as me, but not prettier than me. Besides, I'd need someone to help me kill any others, not that there are very many," Candy spoke her shallow thought process, as it came to her. The two girls burst into a fit of giggles at their own wit. Too bad the joke wasn't funny.

"Especially the two in the car with us," Annie whispered, even though everyone heard what she had said.

It wasn't as if they were driving in a limousine, and the driver could separate them from the passenger with a partition. If they could not have heard them, it might have solved many problem areas in the conversation department, and Pat would definitely have used it.

"Yeah, especially you, Sunny; you have nothing to worry about," Candy added with a giggle, no discretion and a wave with the back of her hand facing upward. She hadn't even tried to hide what she was saying, and Pat was outraged. There was no way she could stand to drive all the way to college with these two bimbos.

Sunny didn't flinch. Her facial expression became hard, but not in a reactive way. Pat wondered if there was steam coming out of her ears, relieving her brain from the fury she must have felt. She pulled the Buick into the service station for gas.

Candy and Annie went off by themselves because they didn't want to be seen in the company of Pat and Sunny. That was the last straw. Pat sat behind the wheel in silence. She knew what she had to do.

Once the Buick's gas tank was full, Pat pulled out of the gas station without the two girls. There was a bus stop across the street, and the bimbos could take the bus. She didn't care how they got to the college, but they weren't going with her. She would refund their money and take their luggage, but that was all.

Sunny grinned, as they headed down the highway. Her facial expression softened.

"Thanks," she said in a gentle voice, as if she were surprised.

"My pleasure," Pat assured her.

They had pushed one too many of her buttons, and the trip wasn't even half over. Sunny opened up after that. She confided in Pat about her gender choice, which was to be gay, and how her parents had always wanted a boy. She mentioned that no matter what she did, she couldn't please them, and she really felt hurt that they didn't love her.

Pat tried to say that she was sure that they loved her, but Sunny assured her that this was not the case because she was female. It saddened Pat to think of the conversation she had been privy to between Sunny's parents. She hoped that Sunny was mistaken, but wasn't sure that she was. Parents should love their children unconditionally.

Her own parents so loved her. Her mother was prim and proper and yet could carry her weight in her field. Her dad was gentle and kind but firm. He leaned more toward the strict side than her mother did, but as long as Pat followed the rules, which she always did, there wasn't a problem. Never once did she feel unloved or neglected in any way.

Sunny had trouble fitting in and making friends because of her looks, and it hurt her so much, she told Pat. She had never let anyone see that before that moment, she added quietly. Pat listened with great sympathy.

Sunny was anything but sunny. She was so sad. Why did society have to be like that? Couldn't they just let people be who they were and be done with it?

CHAPTER TWO

The first freshman semester had gone great, and Pat felt as if she were really on her way. She had met so many new people from every walk of life imaginable. One certain young man had found his way into her very essence at orientation. She had been going through the motions of getting to each class and getting books, paperwork, and meeting the teachers, as expected. She was sitting in psychology class when a young man slid into the seat next to hers. She smiled at him and turned her attention back to the professor to be polite. It was then that the barricade protecting her inner being from the outside world began to break down.

Something about the scene became unbearable for her for some unfathomable reason but in a pleasantly odd way. She smiled to herself in the silent memory, as if she could feel him sitting there beside her. He didn't say a word, but she felt his eyes bore through her each second that passed. He got inside her core without the needed map. She tried with all her might not to pay attention to the unsettling warmth filling her insides.

It was unlike anything that she had ever experienced before, and all he was doing was sitting next to her and looking at her. It was more that he seemed to look through her. It was uncomfortably nice.

As much as she fought the sensation, she was unable to overtake it, and finally, she turned toward him a little to try to sneak a peek at him. She looked right into his huge grinning face and felt the blood rush to her face. She was embarrassed, but had no idea why she would be embarrassed. She hadn't done or said anything wrong, and neither had he.

She fumbled with her pen and papers and then looked in his direction accidentally to see if he was still grinning. He was. It was so crazy. Her reaction was that of a thirteen-year-old just discovering the concept of boys being the opposite sex, yet she couldn't control it.

The experience reminded her of that men's cologne commercial on television where this good-looking guy sprayed himself with the cologne and women came over mountains, across oceans, through deserts, and out of every crevasse of the universe just to be with him. She actually wondered if there was such cologne and if it would make females respond in that manner, and if so, was the person sitting next to her wearing it. Her heart was literally racing inside her chest.

Finally, after several minutes seeming like a lifetime had passed, he asked her if she was all right. She tried rather unsuccessfully to calm down, but it was as if she were in a trance of some sort. She remembered giggling, laughing, and twirling her hair to alleviate her nerves. She learned a little about him that day but a lot about herself. Besides becoming a blithering idiot in the presence of someone she would much rather have made the opposite impression on, she learned that she didn't know much about what to do in a situation where she was chemically attracted to, or had a primal attraction to, a person of the opposite sex.

It had never really come up. She'd been on dates, but never once had she reacted like that to any of them. In her opinion, it was pathetic.

She laughed at herself. He had shown up in the class a few times more, each time making her crazy. She found herself thinking about him and decided that it might be better if she did not see him again, at least not until her senior year. Perhaps he would not audit the second required psychology course, but who knew for sure? She wasn't sure which she truthfully wanted. It depended on the moment. She was glad for the upcoming winter break.

It was the holiday season, and she was going to drive the Buick home for the holidays. Sunny would accompany her. Candy and Annie had requested safe passage ALL the way home as well. Pat conceded to the request with the explicit instructions that they were not to speak, and they had agreed.

As it turned out, the college crowd had seen through the high school princess façade and deemed the duo very ugly people. It was poetic justice in Pat's mind, as well as the truth. The two girls complied with the demand, and they were dropped off safely on the front steps of their homes. Sunny's house was next. The two girls, now good friends, sped off toward their destination.

As they drove past the little strip of stores in the town square where Sunny lived, Pat noticed a police officer giving a bag to a homeless man. In her mind, she silently pitied the poor destitute person. It was so sad that even in this toppling economy, people had to suffer like that. She took comfort that the officer was helping the guy out. Sunny interrupted her thoughts, as they were getting very close to her house.

Sunny confided in Pat about the anxiety she was feeling on her arrival home. Ralph and Tiffany-Crystal always made her feel so out of place. College had been good for Sunny. There was a melting pot of differences in the people residing there, and it seemed as if anything was okay. Okay for Sunny was the closest thing she had ever felt to being accepted.

Pat confided to Sunny that she, too, had a little animosity about going home. Her mother was fixing her up with some friend's son. She did it often, and it made Pat crazy. Her parents wanted her to marry a clean-cut, stable man with a good job and make many babies. Her mother's job had allowed for that, but Pat's chosen career wouldn't be quite as forgiving. Before she even thought about marriage, she wanted to finish college and try her hand at the job she would pick as a forensic scientist. Her parents couldn't comprehend that for some reason, and now, she was stuck going out on this blind date.

Pat scrunched her face up in a distorted manner, and both girls shivered at the thought. As a rule, blind dates were never good, and if your mother set it up, it was sure to be beyond the worst date in the history of dates. Sunny understood. Her mother had also pulled that stunt a time or two.

As they pulled into Sunny's driveway, Pat could see the expression on her face change. She was home. She sighed heavily, and they got out of the car simultaneously. Pat helped Sunny bring her things in. She was not surprised to find the scene the exact same way she had left it. Ralph was in the recliner; his disgusting friend was on the love seat; and Tiffany-Crystal was serving pigs in a blanket to them merrily.

"Oh, hello, dear, you're home early," Tiffany-Crystal sang out. She put the tray on the end table next to Ralph who demanded another beverage right away. Tiffany-Crystal did, as she was ordered, like an obedient puppy dog.

"Actually, I'm late," Sunny said in a monotone voice.

Her eyes then focused on her mother for the first time. Something about her was desperately wrong.

"Are you okay, Mom?" Sunny asked, looking closer at her mother. Pat looked at Tiffany-Crystal. She had bags under her eyes and looked tired. She seemed puffy compared to the last time that she'd seen her. She figured that Tiffany-Crystal was most likely in a womanly way and perhaps not feeling her best.

"She's fine, aren't you, cupcake?" Ralph grunted and slapped her hard on the behind.

Sunny looked appalled. Pat felt that way. Tiffany-Crystal just giggled. Pat was glad to say good-bye to the family of her friend and be on her way. She almost wanted to bring Sunny with her to save her from them. The smiling snowman on the snowy blanket that was the front lawn seemed far luckier than Sunny was. Pat would have dated him if it hadn't been for the fix-up waiting for her at home. The snowman probably had more in common with her. She sighed and continued homeward.

CHAPTER THREE

On the way back to college for the second semester, she picked Sunny up again. Tiffany-Crystal was all made up in her usual primped style, but she looked as if she was going to be ill any second. She looked even puffier than she had the month before. Pat wondered if she was all right and decided to ask Sunny once they were in the car.

"How's your mom doing?" Pat asked concerned, as they drove out on to the icy highway toward Annie and Candy's neighborhood.

"Dad's been on her pretty bad about her weight. She gained ten pounds, and she says that she doesn't know why. To be honest, I don't know why, either. She eats like a bird," Sunny said with a shrug.

Pat realized that Tiffany-Crystal must have built the snowman to get a break from Ralph or perhaps for a workout to keep her figure intact, but she decided not to add that thought to the conversation. Adding fuel to these emotional demon-filled hot embers might cause a fire that could not be contained in her friend.

"I think that he's picking on her because I'm not there," Sunny added, as her eyes met the floor.

Pat felt bad. She recognized and had now grown to loathe that submissive, helpless tone Ralph brought out in his womenfolk. Sunny obviously loved her mother very much, although she felt unworthy of that love being returned. Intense pain radiated from her.

Pat listened to Sunny tell her all the horrible things Ralph had said and done to her throughout her life because she was so ugly. He'd only wanted a boy. Tiffany had not argued a different side at all. She was a disappointment right from birth, and then her looks had sealed her fate with them. Being perky and bouncy wasn't her style, not that it would fit her body type if she were.

"Talk about getting the worst of both sides," Sunny said, picturing herself in a little goofy dress serving pigs in a blanket, and then describing the scene to Pat. Pat nodded and let a little chuckle escape.

"I like you just the way you are," she assured Sunny.

"You like me even though I'm gay?" Sunny asked her directly. The question startled Pat. She had been told by Sunny that she was gay, but had not given it a second throught. She had forgotten because it hadn't mattered. She recovered quickly without saying so.

"I don't care if you are if you don't care that I'm not," Pat replied truthfully with an uncommitted shrug.

"No, I don't mind," Sunny answered the unasked question about friendship that lay underneath what was being verbalized.

No one had ever responded the way Pat had to the news before. It took Sunny a second to wrap her mind around it. Her gender choice was not, nor would it ever become, a problem between them as friends.

"By the way, how did the date go?" Sunny asked, as they drove on.

"Don't ask," Pat replied in an over exaggeratedly exasperated tone and rolled her eyes.

Sunny waited anxiously for the punch line. She knew that there had to be one. Blind dates always had a punch line. It was the only way to survive them without sticking your head in the mud and hiding like an ostrich.

"Let's just say that Chucky Cheese had nothing on this guy. They could've been twins, except that old Chucky would've been more interesting to talk to," Pat added. Sunny grinned and pictured the well-known character from her favorite childhood food chain.

"And Chucky cooks well too," she agreed, straight-faced with a nod of approval.

Sunny laughed, unable to hold the emotion back and so did Pat, as they rounded the corner in the small town holding the college campus. There was no question. The date had been a complete disaster. They had called it. The punch line proved it.

Pat glanced over at a crowd that seemed to have caught Sunny's attention. Sunny craned her neck to see what they were doing, so Pat slowed the car down a bit. There was a police officer standing in a crowd of homeless people. It looked as if he were handing out coffee and donuts to the grateful people. Pat couldn't help admire the officer. It was a nice thing he was doing, but it didn't seem as if it should capture Sunny's attention to the degree it did.

"What are you looking at?" Pat asked, unsure if the scene was the same thing that her friend was studying.

"Nothing; I just thought that I recognized... No, it couldn't be," Sunny answered, shaking her head.

Pat looked at her blankly. She had no clue what Sunny was talking about. Her words were presented in a fragmented sentence emulating her thought process, but something was lost in the translation.

"What?" Pat asked, making a wry face that pleaded for clarification. Should she stop? Which homeless person did

Sunny think that she knew? Could she do anything? From
the back of the car, Candy and Annie swooned at the police
officer's physique. You'd have thought that they'd spotted a
movie star or something. Pat couldn't help notice that too. She
wondered what his face looked like, but they didn't have a clear
view.

"It's not who I thought it was." Relief found its way into
Sunny's reply. Pat was just as glad because she was tired and
wanted to get situated in her dorm room so that she could rest.

She sped up a bit and the road back to the campus
loomed before them in a welcoming manner. They were glad
to be back at school, as they pulled the Buick up to the curb
to unload all their items. Life back at the college would be
a wonderful change. It was almost as if they'd grown up too
much to depend on their mommies and daddies over the first
semester. It was great to be back on their own, making their
own decisions again. It was time to get back to the business of
studying.

CHAPTER FOUR

Pat sat in class and let her mind wander toward her future for a minute. It looked bright. She came to the college to study forensic pathology, hoping to join the law enforcement officials in bringing the guilty to justice and setting the innocent free. She was doing very well in the field and learning so much about it. Psychology was a course also required to get her degree. She had aced the first psychology course and was now settled in the more advanced training needed for her degree. She forced herself back into the classroom situation. High grades were necessary for her future to remain the same, as her dreams would have it be.

The students had been back at school for about two months. Throughout the course, she wondered often why she had to be in the class in the first place. It all seemed like common sense to her. It was her given opinion that science could, and would, tell her all she needed to know on any given case. Forensic evidence was the key, not psychology. Common sense was not something she believed was lacking in her personality.

Her mind could not seem to focus on what was going on in class. She thought of that guy she'd met at orientation, again throughout the first semester's psychology class, and periodically this semester in the new class, and she wondered if she'd ever see him again. He wasn't her usual type, but something about him drew her in. It was almost as if he gave off a primal compelling scent or something like that, that she couldn't resist. Now, there was a question for the psychology professor. Why was she so crazed every time he came within ten feet of her?

They had discussed the most invasive procedures in lab class together. He had been auditing the class again that day. She hadn't even gotten his name yet. She was too foolish every time he came in to remember to get it, yet she could carry on an entire conversation requiring intelligence with him. It was so weird.

The voice of the psychology professor sifted through the barrier wall guarding her brain from learning, and she heard the end of the lesson being taught. It pulled her back from her thoughts and into the reality of the classroom. What he was saying was new and interesting.

"Homeostasis can be described as reactions to certain influences. For instance, the retina of an eye reacts to light, enabling it to process visual information; blood sugars in the body are balanced the same way. Homeostatic behaviors create a balance of power in the human psyche. The human feels the sense of belonging or fitting into a "norm." It's an organized fully rounded state of mind in a healthy form," the professor defined.

"Take me, for instance; my mother was the one everybody in town came to if they needed to talk to someone. She was the town yenta. Everyone loved her. My father was a doctor. His bedside manner was impeccable, and his patients adored him. Is it any wonder then that I, as their only child, would become a psychologist? It is in my homeostatic nature to help people learn and deal with life's patterns and the reasons they occur. Naturally, my pathway then took me to the level of teacher. One can find a pattern of homeostasis in most every area," the professor lectured.

"If that is the case, then why do people commit horrible crimes, suicide, or murder?" One student questioned the logic the professor was trying to get across to his class.

"Ah, yes, that is a good question. In some families, homeostasis can become severely unhealthy. Cases such as an abused child growing up and entering an abusive relationship or abusing their own children are common," the professor began.

"But what about a typically normal family where the child grows up to commit rape or murder—what happened to homeostatic behavior there?" another student questioned.

"That's where the factor of human interpretation comes in," the professor said with a fulfilled grin. He loved teaching to an interested group.

"Each human has the gift of free will. Each interprets things differently. In simple form, we can use the half-full glass of water. Some see it as half full; others see it as half empty; and others will see a dirty glass or a clean one; yet others will notice bubbles in the water or clear water. Do you see what I mean? We are all seeing the same glass," he continued.

A murmur spread through the classroom. Interpretations of what the professor said varied, almost proving his point on the spot. Pat thought about her own life for a moment. Her father was a decorated detective in the Federal Bureau of Investigation, well-respected and a force to be reckoned with. Her mother was a science teacher. She was kind, gentle, and quiet, but a force to be reckoned with in a different way. Her force was quiet—a gentle kind of strength.

Pat had entered the world of forensic science. She, too, could be a force to be reckoned with when she got her dander up or be opinionated in a quiet reserved way if she needed to. She laughed a little bit. Homeostasis appeared to be accurate, at least where she was concerned.

"Your theme project for the semester is unhealthy homeostasis. You must show research backed up with cases already logged on subjects such as abuse, murder, rape, and the like, and then form a conclusive opinion. I do not want abnormal psychology. We will discuss actual illness later," the professor said, as the bell rang signifying the end of the class.

Once again, murmurs filled the room discussing the clinical project, as everyone filed out the door. It mesmerized Pat as the most interesting thing she believed had gone on in the class so far. It excited her, and she tossed around ideas in her head on what subject she would focus on for the project. She was positive that the right subject would allow her limited forensic knowledge to be brought in as evidence to her conclusion.

CHAPTER FIVE

A crowd had formed outside the dorm where Pat stayed with other college students. She had just gotten out of her psychology class, and she was dragging her heels from exhaustion due to thinking about a subject for her project. She noticed the head of her friend Sunny sticking out above the rest of the crowd and headed toward her to get the scoop about what was going on. "What's up?" she asked Sunny, looking at the growing crowd. Sunny shrugged her huge shoulders, and her face grimaced in confusion. Pat couldn't help grin. Seeing Sunny confused was an unusual sight.

Sunny was still no less than six-foot-three and weighing in at a petite two hundred and fifty pounds. She had short buzz cut hair that looked as if it had a tint of red in it put there purposefully, since it hadn't been there before now. Her eyes were too small for her face and blue in color.

The difference was that she was now a very strong, very focused person who was a self-proclaimed lesbian and proud to be so. She worked at the construction site of the strip mall going up a few blocks from the college when she wasn't in architecture classes. She had changed for the better by being at the college.

"I have no idea," Sunny answered, looking around for some hint in the crowd.

The Dean of Students came by and asked the crowd to disperse and everyone to go to their rooms and wait for further instruction. His face was twisted with worry lines. The classes for the rest of the day were then cancelled. That's when everyone knew there was a problem.

As Pat walked down the hallway to her room, she could hear screaming. Someone was completely freaking out. Many official people went in and out of a room down the hall. The students all whispered to each other along the way. Some knew more than others did. The story came out in spurts.

It seemed that the officer monitoring the police emergency number picked up the receiver on her end to the distraught hysteria of a female voice. Through sobs and tears, the young woman on the other end of the line gave her name and address to the officer. She tried unsuccessfully to describe the scene she had walked into on arriving back at the dorm. The officer immediately dispatched law enforcement to the scene.

The dorm swarmed with police, forensic pathologists, an ambulance, and medical examiners. Onlookers were held at bay, as the officials went through the crime scene with a careful precision. Police questioned the young woman who had made the call, as she sat in a room adjoining where the crime had taken place, wrapped up in a blanket, as she answered to the best of her ability between sobs.

CHAPTER SIX

"The victim was her roommate," an older officer explained to his new partner inside the perimeter of the crime scene. The rookie listened in wide-eyed shock, as the older officer took off his hat and scratched his silver hair. The rookie noticed the pallor forming in the cheeks of his seasoned partner. The aging man wiped his reddening blue eyes with his shirtsleeve, as creases formed deep crevices across his brow. "This type of thing never ceases to amaze me," he admitted to the rookie with a quiet voice.

The rookie knew that his partner had seen many horrific crimes in his twenty-five years on the force. The rookie said nothing of his observation. He had big dreams of seeing the same and much, much more. He believed that his contribution would be of epic proportion, bringing the world to its knees at his grandeur.

Still, it was as if the older officer became somewhat older in the few minutes he described the crime, trying to prepare his young protégé for the crime scene he was about to see. The rookie's heart softened for the old-timer. Perhaps age had taken away the edge he'd had in his youth. Perhaps the time to retire was drawing near.

He put his aged hand reassuringly on the shoulder of his rookie partner. The rookie could feel the warm sweat seep through the cloth of his uniform shirt and onto his skin. He nodded. He felt as ready as he ever would be. He wondered what was beyond the doorframe that had upset the older officer so much, given that he'd seen so much in his career. Whatever it was, he couldn't believe that it was that heinous.

He took a deep breath, as his partner turned to enter the scene with a solemn look on his face. The rookie stepped lightly, as if no sound coming from his shoes on the tiled floor might help him stay hidden from the fear. It welled up inside him, as he approached his first real crime scene as an officer of the law.

The room was small and very crowded. The officials on the scene seemed to lurk around the bed. His elderly partner stepped slightly to the side, and he got a full view of the first murder scene he would ever witness as a police officer in charge of solving the crime.

A young woman lay on her bed. The blanket underneath her looked as if she'd just climbed back into an unmade bed. The woman had long, yellow blond hair with dark roots, and it was wet. Her body had blotches of blue that looked as if she were bruising, and her lips were a dark purple-blue color. The girl was naked to her waist with her left thumb in her mouth. She was wearing a diaper made of a pillowcase. Pillows were on each side of her, the way one might put them next to a baby if one were afraid the baby might roll off the bed. She had been petite and beautiful when she was alive; there was no question in the rookie's mind about that. He wanted to know exactly what they knew. He wanted to know the facts.

"Her hair is wet?" the rookie half asked his partner with a hoarse voice. He wondered if that was the base for the smell enveloping the room like a thick shroud. His stomach began churning, and for a moment, he thought he might hurl. The smell was not something he had expected.

"The perpetrator bathed her, lotioned her, and powdered her," one official working the scene answered.

"And he closed her eyes," a woman officer commented with a gentle tone.

"I think she was drowned in the bathtub first. I'll have more after we autopsy her," the medical examiner added.

"That doesn't smell like lotion," the rookie said. His face seemed to turn a weird shade of green underneath the pallor. No one acknowledged the statement, as the investigation and evidence gathering continued.

"Her name is LuAnn Shelby. She just turned twenty-one last night. Her friend Natalie saw her leave the party with a man. We're bringing in the police artist now," one detective mentioned.

"Lu was such a good person. We've been roommates here at the college for three years now," Natalie was saying through sobs.

The rookie turned around to look at Natalie, as she spoke. Her face was as red as an apple, and tears flowed from her eyes like a river breaking through a dam. He knew that those eyes had seen something they'd never forget. His stomach churned again. It was the stench engulfing the scene. He hadn't smelled anything like it before. Sweat filled his upper lip, and he wiped it away.

"You okay, kid?" his partner asked. The rookie nodded. The aroma in the room was overwhelming him. It was a ghastly sickening stench making his eyes water.

"Drown victims smell the worst of all of them. It's not something they can teach you at the academy. You have to experience it to know," the older officer whispered to the rookie.

"We're going to have a rough time getting any DNA off this victim. She was washed thoroughly. With the addition of the lotion and powder, we might be out of luck," another frustrated official chimed in.

"It looks as though the perpetrator treated her lovingly, as if she were a baby," the first official agreed.

"Great, a murderer who loves you," one officer joked callously.

"Yeah, that gives a whole new meaning to love them and leave them," another said sarcastically.

The rookie was glad that Natalie could not hear what the people he was associated with were saying. The words made him feel even sicker. Little blue dots started flying around in front of his eyes. His stomach churned vigorously. "Tom, I need to get some air," the rookie said to his older partner, nearly choking out the words.

Without waiting for approval, he darted for the door and ran down the hall to find a bathroom. He put his hand across his mouth to try to hold back the oncoming convulsion that would most likely cost him his lunch and turned a corner at about ninety miles per hour.

He spotted a trashcan and dove for it. His body convulsed until there was nothing left in him, but sympathy for Natalie and what could only be described as pity for LuAnn Shelby, the sweet twenty-one year old girl who allegedly met the wrong man on her birthday.

What would a perpetrator have been trying to prove by doing that to her? What would be written in the "comments" section of the police reports? The rookie thought hard, as he composed himself after the stomach fury that had gone unmatched in his life to date. He needed to be precise. He didn't want to skip a beat more in the investigation if it could be helped. He was determined to be an integral part of solving it, if not the one who solved the case. He would be the one to come up with the answers.

"Are you all right officer?" A friendly female voice asked from behind him, interrupting his train of thought.

"I'm okay," the rookie said composing himself further. She handed him some tissue from her purse, as he stood up.

"Thank you, miss," he said, pausing for a name to be given to his would-be rescuer.

"Farmer, Patricia Farmer; my friends call me Pat," she answered with a smile.

"Thanks, Pat," he said, wiping his mouth.

"You're here because of Natalie, right?" Pat asked with a look of genuine concern on her pretty face.

Pat was blond and small. She had big aqua blue eyes that looked as if they had stolen the color directly from the ocean. Her hair was a tussle of bouncy little curls, and her smile was pearly white against lips that needed no lipstick to be luxurious. Her eyelashes were thick and black. The rookie could not help be awestruck at how perfect she looked in her tiny miniskirt and the sweater that showed just a hint of her navel.

"Do you know anything about Natalie?" The rookie answered her question with another question, and inwardly, he kicked himself for not wording it properly.

"I heard her screaming. We all did. Then, the police showed up, and the Dean told us to stay in our rooms. When we were excused from classes, we knew something was very wrong. Is Natalie okay?" Pat asked.

The rookie knew not to say anything; everything screamed at him from within to keep his mouth shut. For some reason, he could not contain his words.

"She's fine. It's her roommate that is the subject of our investigation," he sputtered.

"Is Lu okay?" Pat gasped.

She and LuAnn had become late night library buddies. They had deep talks about life and confided private thoughts to each other. Pat was set completely off balance by the news that something might be wrong with her.

"I'm not at liberty to say, but I think you should stay in your room and lock the door tonight," the rookie answered.

"I will; thank you, officer." She grabbed her chest and then paused, unexpectedly waiting for a name.

"Officer Cameron Scott, my friends call me Cameron," the rookie stuttered.

"Thank you, Cameron," Pat said, asserting herself as a possible friend, and hurried back into her room past a few closed doors down the hall.

Cameron watched her scurry down the hall. He couldn't help think that even her walk was adorable. He loved the sway of her skirt, as she moved. He threw the tissue in the trash receptacle and tied the bag tightly to contain any smell. He left the bag in place so that the investigation would not be compromised in any way.

Pat sat at her desk. She wondered what had happened to Lu. She wondered if Natalie was all right. The officer had sounded so solemn in his inability to disclose information about LuAnn. She wondered if LuAnn had been hurt or raped. What if it was worse? She shook her head and pushed her curls back, filling her lungs with a deep breath of oxygen. She decided not to let her imagination run away with her. She would wait for the facts. It was what a proper forensic scientist would do. Speculation wouldn't cut it in a field where solid evidence would show itself eventually.

Her mind drifted to the young male officer who had lost his lunch over whatever he had seen in LuAnn and Natalie's room. He was tall, slender, and muscular. He had brown clean-cut hair and beautiful big brown eyes. He was obviously sensitive; his actions by the trash pail had proven that.

"Officer Cameron Scott," she said aloud. "Am I your friend? Can I call you Cameron again, and stick around next time?" she asked the memory fanning out in her mind, and she wondered if she'd get the chance to see him again.

ews of LuAnn's death spread like wildfire across the
college campus. Everyone was in an uproar about it.
Everyone was in fear. Everyone wondered who would
do such a thing to her. Pat had felt from their first meeting as
dorm mates that she really was a nice person.

Often people glorify the memory of the dead by painting a
rosier picture of what the person was like when they were alive,
but not in this case. LuAnn had been a sweet, conservative,
hard worker who was only out to better herself. Pat had
become fast friends with LuAnn, and the news hit her hard.

LuAnn had come from poverty and clawed her way up
to where she was when an unknowing, heartless assailant cut
her life short. Sarcastically, Pat asked herself what homeostatic
pattern the culprit that took LuAnn's life was like. It was
definitely unhealthy. She wished she could do something to
help. Standing around helpless wasn't her style. She needed to
participate actively in the apprehension of the murderer. She
wasn't one for letting someone else handle it, especially because
LuAnn had become her friend.

"Maybe that's the unhealthy side of my homeostatic
pattern," she spoke aloud, though no one was with her to hear
her words. She gasped at her own thoughts.

She felt as if a light bulb went off in her brain lighting up
all the corners full of dusty cobwebs. A plan began shaping
in her mind. She would use the death of her friend as her
psychology project. She could also assist with the forensic
evidence, gaining first-hand experience at the job she hoped

to be doing one day, as well as helping to catch the horrible person who committed the crime against her friend. She was sure that an unhealthy homeostatic pattern would show itself. All kinds of papers had been written about murderers and their victims. Research would not be a problem. She would approach her professor with the idea right away.

She sat in lab and tapped her foot incessantly waiting for the time to pass. It seemed to be dragging on and on endlessly. She'd get through it, but the task was difficult. The disappearing guy, as she had come to think of him, whom she had met several classes before, claiming to audit it, angled into the chair next to her. Her heart immediately began beating a little faster at the sight of him. Perhaps it was that undetectable primal scent again. He was apparently going to audit the end of class again and chose to sit next to her as he had every other time.

Momentarily, she wondered why he was allowed to do that, but her thoughts veered to the left, as he spoke. Her stomach seemed to go into some kind of a little frenzy when he sat down. His arm brushed up against her, as she inhaled a breath, and she found herself in the position of not being able to exhale the same breath. Her reactions were untamed and wild. She thought that it was odd, but said nothing about it to him, of course.

"Did you hear about the girl killed on campus?" he whispered. She nodded, facing him. He now had her full attention. What was going on with her heartbeat? She wondered if he could see it beating beneath her blouse. She rested her hand over it in case. It was unusual to say the least. She shook the thought off, as he continued.

"Look at these," he said, pulling some photos out of his bag. They were pictures of LuAnn. She was lying on a stainless steel slab. She was obviously at the morgue. Pat was horrified but able to control her expression.

"Where did you get these?" she asked him in astonishment.

"I have my ways," he said, raising his eyebrows.

He slid out of the chair, as the instructor dismissed the class. Pat felt frozen to her spot.

What kind of morbid curiosity must that guy have to sneak into a morgue and take pictures of her deceased dorm mate? He claimed to want to be a medical examiner. She guessed that this was why he had done it. Still, this wasn't just anyone. LuAnn was someone she knew, someone she liked. A shiver ran up her spine.

She walked at a quick pace toward the psychology offices where she hoped to find her professor and address her idea. She hoped that he would pull strings in the campus police department to get her a spot on the team working the murder case, preferably in the forensics lab.

Pat spotted Sunny sitting on the edge of the fountain in the middle of the campus grounds. Her friend looked as if she were upset about something. She swerved from her path over to Sunny, even though she knew that time was an element she was limited on at the moment.

"Hey, Sunny; what's up? I haven't seen you much lately," Pat called out. Sunny looked up and smiled upon recognizing her friend.

"Mom sent pictures from home," Sunny said, holding them up. There were three. Sunny shoved one in her pocket, explaining it to be an awful picture of her. One photo was of Ralph and his vile friend, and one was of Ralph and Tiffany-Crystal.

Tiffany-Crystal was bent over behind the recliner with her face tucked low to fit into the picture. She was holding a tray of food off to the side and smiling big. Her face looked rounder than Pat had remembered it to be. Tiffany-Crystal was also supporting a double chin.

"I bet Ralph is torturing her over the weight gain," Sunny commented sadly. She knew very well how hard Ralph could be on a person that didn't meet his standards, especially if that person was a female.

"He's fat and ugly himself. He has no right to say anything to your mother," Pat agreed, looking at the foul male with the half-smoked stogie hanging out of his mouth.

"That doesn't stop him. She's not tough like me. She's not used to being treated like that. I don't think she can take it," Sunny said.

Pat could see the sadness and torment radiating through Sunny's eyes. Though the word tough was not how she would've described Sunny, she understood what she meant by it. She'd place a bet on Tiffany-Crystal being depressed and gaining weight because the only comfort she got was from chocolate.

It was the way of the modern world. Obesity was running rampant, and depression often went hand in hand with the problem. A person ate to comfort the depression, gained weight, and became more depressed, only to need comfort again. It was a vicious circle.

A piercing shriek interrupted the girls' conversation. Both Pat and Sunny ran toward the scream without hesitation. It had come from a dorm close by.

They ran into the building, looking around frantically for which room it had come from. The elevator opened, and a disheveled, crying female emerged from behind the doors. She had dark skin, dark hair, red eyes, and red lips.

"It's Bobbie. I think she's dead," the girl spoke through raging sobs.

"Which room?" Pat asked.

"Two twenty three, on the second floor," the girl answered with tears streaking violent jagged lines down her cheeks.

"Go get the police," Pat instructed and then got in the elevator with Sunny, who was already inside and holding the door.

Sunny pressed floor 2, and in seconds, they were at the door of room 223. Pat pushed the door open slowly. The dorm room was small. The walls were pale yellow brick, and two beds were against the sides. Each bed had a dresser, a desk, and a chair for the student living there. In one bed, a female lay very still. She seemed to be sucking her thumb and wearing a diaper made from a bathroom towel. She had pillows tucked around her that looked like protection, as if she were going to fall off the bed. Her eyes, too, were closed.

"Oh, gees," Pat said in a gasp and held her hand up to her mouth.

Sunny just stood there stone-faced. Neither female could believe their eyes. It was a dead person. Another murder had taken place on campus. Police sirens sounded in the distance.

Once law officials arrived, the two females were questioned thoroughly and then ushered from the crime scene. A female officer accompanied in Kathy, Bobbie's roommate. The rookie, Cameron Scott, was there with his partner, and an array of other law enforcement officials paraded in and out.

Pat's jaw dropped in shock, as she watched the male stranger who had showed her photos from the morgue walk in undetected by anyone. No one stopped him or even said anything. He put his finger to his lips as if to tell Pat not to say anything, as he wandered right into the crime scene. She couldn't believe her eyes. Was he getting some perverse pleasure out of seeing dead bodies? Another shiver went up her spine. What was it that plagued her about him?

Once Pat was back in her dorm, she headed straight for her room. She ran into Candy and Annie in the hallway.

"Did you hear about Barbara McIntyre?" Annie asked her. Pat nodded. She didn't feel like discussing what she had seen first hand.

"Well, it doesn't surprise me," Candy added, trying to pass along gossip.

"What doesn't surprise you?" Pat asked, taking the bait and immediately regretting it.

"That someone would want to kill her, stupid; she was so conceited. She thought she was so beautiful," Annie explained, rolling her eyes as if Pat were an idiot.

Pat couldn't believe her ears. She pushed past the bimbos and continued toward her room. How could they be so clueless? A human was murdered, and they made it seem like no big deal. She couldn't believe what small, shallow minds they had.

"Oh, go look in a mirror, will you?" Pat sneered at them through her teeth. Instead of getting the message, she heard them questioning each other about their makeup, as they fled down the hall to fix whatever was wrong with their faces. When Pat got to her room, she closed the door and locked it behind her.

She was alone in the room because her roommate had failed out in the first semester. She had felt so lonely at first, but she was glad to be alone now. She didn't want to be with anyone else just then.

That was the last straw. She was going to her psychology teacher right after class in the morning. If he wouldn't help her, then she'd ask the weird stranger who kept turning up. That guy seemed to be able to get into any place he wanted.

She wondered how he'd gained access. If she couldn't do it the right way, she intended to do it any way. She flung herself on her bed and stared at the ceiling. It didn't hurt that he was so cute, either, with his jet-black locks and huge coal black eyes. He was the mysterious, dark stranger in her life. Part of her liked it, even though warning whistles were blasting in her head, and flags were going up at every turn.

The next morning, the murder was all over the campus and all over the news. The headlines called the crimes "The Baby Diaper Murders." The description fit. The police were afraid of a serial killer being on the loose and were running down leads on what the two victims might have had in common.

According to the newspaper, Barbara, known to her friends as Bobbie, was a sophomore. She was studying liberal arts, and she worked as a server at The Little Lunch House diner close to the school. She was an exemplary student who attended church every Sunday and came from a strong middle-class background.

The only two things the victims seemed to have in common were that they both attended the same college, and they were both petite females. Nothing else before the murders came up as a match. The murders, however, were the same each time.

Identity Theft: It's Murder!

CHAPTER EIGHT

Pat sat through psychology class, but did not gain an ounce of knowledge from it. All she could think about was the need to be part of solving the Baby Diaper Murders. When class finally ended, she felt as though she might burst. She approached the teacher who promised that he would check into her request.

On the way back to her dorm, she spotted a crowd over by the lounge. Something inside of her became uneasy. Sensing another problem, she turned from her path and veered toward the crowd. Police had blocked off the area. The coroner's van and law vehicles filled the area just seconds behind Pat's arrival on the scene.

"What's going on?" Sunny's familiar voice asked from behind her.

"I don't know. Can you see anything?" Pat asked.

Sunny stood on her toes and was able to get a good idea of what was going on.

"It looks as if someone was murdered in the lounge this time," she speculated.

Sunny described the scene taking place, as she watched. A gurney was pushed out of the lounge with a person wrapped up in a black bag. Pat listened in horror. Annie came out with a blanket wrapped around her shoulders. She was clearly sobbing.

"What about Candy? Do you see her? They are always together," Pat asked. Sunny shook her head no and searched for her again. She scanned the area a third time. Candy was nowhere in sight.

"What's going on?" a high-pitched soprano voice asked, as Pat and Sunny continued to look intensely for Candy.

"We're not sure," Sunny said with the words cutting off abruptly. The color drained from her face. She tapped Pat on the shoulder. Pat turned to look Candy right in the face.

"Candy, thank heaven you're okay," Pat gushed, genuinely relieved to see her.

"Why wouldn't I be?" Candy asked, annoyed by the show of affection.

"Annie is with the police. A body was just taken from the lounge," Sunny explained hoarsely. Now, it was Candy's turn to gasp.

"I was supposed to meet her here after class." Candy explained why the two were not yet together.

Pat got a clear view of the guy who had infiltrated the other death scenes. He seemed to look right at her with a huge grin before the crowd closed around her again. When the group dispersed, the guy was gone. Pat wanted to talk to him. She wanted to know how he had gotten into the center of each scene. It infuriated her and frustrated her. Here she was trying to go through the proper channels, and he just waltzed right in. It was unfair.

Later, they found that Annie had discovered the third body. Several suites were just off the back of the lounge. Annie had gone to one suite to retrieve a bracelet she had lost and found the victim. Instead of getting her bracelet, she got a nightmare that would forever torment her. This was getting too close for comfort.

The victim's name was Jacqueline Stockbridge. She was found in the same position as the two other girls had been found. She had dark hair and hazel eyes. She was studying as a business major, and she had taken a secretarial position at an insurance company in town to pay the bills. Pat and Sunny did not know her, but the consensus among those that did was that she was a nice person. She'd have given the shirt off her back to anyone in need, and she was a kind decent person.

It also came out that she'd recently had an abortion. No one knew who the father was but had seen her with a man matching the police artist description shown to all the students on campus. Pat wondered openly if the abortion factor could be the link connecting the victims. They seemed posed purposely to look like a baby, in her opinion. She decided to go find Officer Cameron Scott and raise the question.

She wanted to see him again. This not only gave her a reason, but she hoped that he might help her get in on the investigation if she mentioned it. It couldn't hurt to try from two separate angles after all, she surmised.

At least she was trying to do it legitimately, unlike whatever his name was. She made a silent promise to get the guy's name next time the chance presented itself, no matter how fragile her brain became—not knowing it was dumber than dumb, in her opinion.

Pat now had a purpose. She excused herself less than gracefully from the most current scene, as only stragglers were left, and scurried off to her dorm room. She wanted to deposit her backpack and change her clothes before going downtown to see Cameron Scott and give him the new information she had inadvertently uncovered.

She gave her hair one last fluff in the mirror, grabbed her purse, and headed out the door toward the parking lot. As she reached the Buick, the guy who had gotten an inside glimpse at the murders and vital information at all the crime scenes called out to her.

"Hey, you," he yelled, and she looked directly toward where the shouting had come from.

She turned and saw the mysterious, dark stranger, and her heart began racing on cue. It was an unexplainable phenomenon. Her brain began to fog. She grabbed a lock of hair, twirled it nervously, and then realized that she was going into bimbo mode again. She stopped herself abruptly, reminding herself to get his name this time.

What was happening to her here had to be a psychological phenomenon of some sort. She decided that she would study it one day. It bore scrutiny. She tried to compose herself. She hoped that he didn't notice.

"Hey, yourself," she called back, putting one hand over her eyes to block the sun from impairing her view.

"I never got your name," he said, approaching her.

"Patricia Farmer," she said, sticking out her hand in a businesslike manner for him to shake it.

"And you are?" she asked.

"Tony Bensoia," he said with a grin. He shook her hand but held it too long. She fought to control the frenzy building inside her.

"Tony, I've been meaning to ask you how you came to have access to the crime scenes of the Baby Diaper Murders," she mentioned without caution. She had all she could do to remember to say it at all.

She felt proud of herself. She'd gotten the two most important things out before the usual meltdown took place, but she could feel it trying to overtake her brain. She fought to control her racing heartbeat. She wanted to get right to the point before she lost track of what the point was.

"I just walk in and act like I'm supposed to be there," he shrugged, as if it were nothing.

"Besides, I work in the security office for the college. They are all so used to seeing me that they don't realize that I'm not supposed to be there," he added smugly.

"I see," she answered without really answering.

It wasn't quite the answer she expected. Somehow, she had romanticized the answer. This answer seemed too plain, considering what she had been experiencing. She heard the hint of disapproval in her own voice and hoped that Tony had not noticed it.

"Where are you off to this fine day?" Tony asked, changing the subject.

Pat decided not to divulge her destination. Something about Tony made her feel very uneasy at the moment. Perhaps it was the change of the flow when he answered her. She couldn't put her finger on it. Perhaps it was just his ability to get into the places that she couldn't. Perhaps it was that her heart raced involuntarily whenever he was around, or perhaps it was the way she felt so unexplainably drawn to him.

"I'm going into town to run some errands," Pat lied.

"Well, I guess I'll see you around then," Tony said in a dismissing tone.

Part of her wondered if he had wanted to join her. He hadn't asked, but perhaps he thought that she would offer. He turned on his heels and headed in the other direction.

She almost felt disappointed at the separation, yet she needed to go see Cameron alone. Pat got into the Buick, gave a friendly wave, and drove off at a slow pace. She wondered why part of her felt like revving the motor and zooming away at full speed, leaving a cloud of dust to cover him in her wake. Why was she reacting so intensely to this guy?

At the police station, there was mayhem. People seemed to be rushing in many directions, and phones rang incessantly. One officer led her to a desk and instructed her to sit down. Officer Scott was due in any time now. She could tell by the secretary's voice that he was late, and no one was happy about it. The secretary escorted her through the abyss of mess and desks. The nameplate on the desk told her that it was Cameron's desk.

The desk, like all the others, was a disheveled pile of files and paperwork. The file on the top was Jacqueline's file. The nickname Jackie was in parentheses underneath her given name. Pat thought about reaching over and flipping it open or at least moving it over to see the files under it. She'd have placed a bet that they were on the other victims of the Baby Diaper Murders. She looked around cautiously. No one seemed to be watching her.

She fixed her position in the chair to reach quickly for the file. It would only take a second. She was going to chance it. Her heart was racing with excitement, and her hand began to move toward the file.

"Patricia Farmer, isn't it? What can I do for you?" Cameron Scott said, coming from behind her and moving around the desk to sit adjacent to her. She put her hand on the desk and fixed her position again, as if that was what she had been doing, instead of committing the illegal act she'd almost been caught doing.

"I'm sorry to be late. I was caught up in traffic," he explained casually.

Pat's breath had been inhaled, but she was unable to exhale for the moment. She felt the blood drain from her brain, and heat filled her cheeks. Had he seen her reach for the file? Did he know she was just about to break the law?

"Are you okay?" he asked with a look of concern crossing his brow. She finally exhaled and then coughed.

"Yes. Maybe I shouldn't have come," she stammered.

He thought that she was the cutest thing he'd ever laid his eyes on. She was clearly uneasy at being in the same room as the police officers. He reveled that he could throw her off like that just by being close to her in his uniform.

"No wait," he said, as she rose from the chair to leave. "You're here now," he said, coaxing her to stay. She nodded, and he smiled genuinely at her.

"I think I have information that you don't have," she tried unsuccessfully to explain.

He allowed a more serious look to mask his face.

"Regarding?" he asked with palms-up motion of his hands.

"About the Baby Diaper Murders case—about Jacqueline," she replied, motioning to the file on his desk absentmindedly. She wanted to kick herself, but he didn't seem to catch the connection, and she was grateful that he obviously hadn't seen her reach for it earlier.

"Did you know her?" Cameron asked, taking out a notebook and pen from his desk drawer.

"No, I didn't, but I know several people that do—did—know her pretty well," Pat said truthfully. How was she going to say this delicately? There was no way. Perhaps she should just blurt it out and be done with it.

"I heard that she'd just had an abortion. The victims' bodies are left as someone might leave a baby. I wondered if the other girls…" She put her theory together in fragmented sentences.

He was greatly pleased that she couldn't look him in the eye and talk of sexual things. In all his twenty-six years of life, he had never met a more adorable female. He decided to let her suffer for another minute or so and then swoop in for the rescue.

"Yes, we know, and we checked out that theory too. The other victims did not have abortions. LuAnn hadn't had sexual intercourse at all, and Bobbi was monogamous with one boyfriend for the past year," Cameron confided quietly, looking directly in her eyes. She turned bright red, and he found the game he was playing with her entrancing.

"Oh," Pat said, feeling disappointment overlaying stupidity. Of course, the police had known, and of course, they had followed up on the possibility that the abortion was the thing the victims had in common. She sighed heavily.

He had all he could do to keep himself composed. She was too innocent to be a college student. How had she gotten to this chronological point in her life without becoming tarnished by some unfeeling cad in high school? Girls like that just weren't real anymore, or so he had thought before now. He was awestruck.

He saw that she was at a loss and wanted to make her feel better. Perhaps he had pressed the innocence she had shown too hard, so he decided to throw her a bone. Another rescue was needed. He decided to play it a little gentler with her.

"I'm impressed that you came up with that, though. Most people would just have kept their mouths shut and stayed away from the situation. Your coming here with information and a theory says something about your character," Cameron assured her.

Her eyes lit up at his compliment. She was easy to manipulate. He was able to push her buttons at will, and it gave him a surge of extraordinary emotion where she was concerned.

"Thank you," Pat said, indeed feeling a little better.

"No, thank you," Cameron said, pointedly stressing the last word. The tone in his voice and the sincerity in his eyes led Pat to believe that he meant what he was saying.

"I have one other question," Pat said quietly.

"Go ahead," he coaxed her further. He was really enjoying this conversation. He wanted to talk to her all day if need be. She fit his unspoken, unthought of plans somehow, even though he hadn't planned on her.

"I've already asked my professor, so now I'll ask you," she began. She explained her project, her career goal, and her reasoning for wanting to be allowed involvement in the Baby Diaper Murders case. Cameron listened.

"I have absolutely no pull here as the new guy, but if I think of something, I'll call you," Cameron promised.

She believed that he would try to help. He seemed like the kind of guy who was down to earth and a man of his word. He was wholesome and refreshing.

He took her dorm phone number, and before she knew what was happening, she was back in the Buick and on her way back to the college. Cameron was only a rookie. She knew that he had no power in getting her into the investigation.

Still, the man now had her phone number, and that was great news. She only hoped that something would happen that would allow her as much access as Tony Bensoia seemed to be privy to.

That wasn't all she hoped would happen. She found herself very attracted to the young officer. His eyes sucked her in with the gravitational pull of a black hole. Her father would be so pleased with his career choice. Her mother would have reveled in his courteous manner. He sure beat the pants off the guys they had fixed her up with previously. She allowed her mind to remember the last guy—Mister Chucky Cheese look-alike—and she was glad to be talking to Cameron instead of him.

She didn't really have to struggle to maintain control and composure around him. Her heart did not race out of control. Instead, it beat in a very pleasant manner. He seemed calm and at ease with her. She wondered if that was a good sign or a bad one. She shook off the thought, as she pulled into a parking space in the lot near her dorm. With a heavy sigh, she got out of the car and locked the door.

CHAPTER NINE

A cross the parking lot, Pat heard shrieks of terror. "Oh no, Please not again. Don't let there be another body," Pat said aloud to herself, as she darted toward the high-pitched screeches.

It couldn't be another body, Pat thought, as she ran. *It's too quick.* The screams were not coming from a dorm. *Could he be escalating?* Another shriek followed. It was coming from the other side of the parking lot. Fear radiated through the voice, as the pitch pierced the atmosphere.

In her recent research concerning serial killers, she had read about the escalation that occurred, as each new murder took place and the killer was not caught. The violence grows, as the rage of the killer's inner beast feeds on itself. He becomes almost cocky in the revelry that the police can never catch him. The fantasies intensify to taunt officials and to satisfy the growing lust for violence. The killer practices at first and becomes better and better. The only good thing about escalating was that this was generally where the killer becomes sloppy and leaves clues behind because he thinks he is above being caught.

By the time Pat arrived at the scene, a crowd had formed. Someone ran off to get campus security, and several others were using cell phones to call the police. Pat gasped. The back of a van was wide open. The sight was enough to turn her hair white. There was indeed another baby diaper murdered body lying in the van on a small blow-up mattress. He had struck again.

The girl in the van was on her side, sucking her thumb and protected by pillows just like the others. She had jet-black hair and dark skin. There was a small diamond nose ring too. She didn't look like any of the others.

"Don't touch anything," Pat yelled and got closer to the crime scene to protect it.

She knew that the perpetrator could have made a mistake this time. This victim was in the back of a van. There was no way she could have been bathed. It was Pat's notion that DNA could be found this time, and the murderer could finally be apprehended.

She stood guard until the police showed up. Tony appeared out of nowhere. He grinned at her, as an older officer ushered her away from the van while he was allowed to remain. He waved without the officer seeing him. It infuriated her.

"There might be DNA. She couldn't have been bathed out here," she spoke quickly to the officer escorting her away.

"Let us handle it, miss," he said authoritatively and handed her over to an officer arriving on the scene.

She watched the police work with animosity. The forensic team showed up, and Tony grinned at her one last time before resuming his close-up view of the latest Baby Diaper Murder victim. She noticed Cameron and his partner arriving on the scene. They both wore ominous looks on their faces, as they began their work. Cameron looked especially tired. His eyes seemed puffy and glassy. Tom didn't look much better.

Minutes later, the camera operator seemed unsteady on his feet for a second before he fainted, as the flashbulb went off. Without thinking, Pat raced to his aid, rescuing the camera before it touched the ground, while he fell on the ground with the help of a nice police officer who caught him as he fell.

A few other officials came in to help him. Pat looked at the camera. It was a Hasselblad, one of the finest cameras in the world of non-digital photography, in her opinion. It was attached to a bracket. She lifted it up to look through the lens.

"Miss, get a photo of this wound," one officer instructed her, not realizing who she was, or rather wasn't, in this case.

At last! A way in had presented itself. She had never used such a magnificent camera before, but had some knowledge of photography as a hobby from her high school days. After playing with it for a moment to get the feel, she went and took the needed photographs, as instructed by the forensic team. She even took a few of her own in the interim so that it looked as though she had photographed murder scenes many times before.

After the work was finished, she gave the camera back to its owner, who was sipping an ice-cold bottle of water, and left her name with him too. She hoped for the photos to turn out good enough for him to allow her to assist if there was a next time. She was desperate to help catch and incarcerate the perpetrator of the heinous, humiliating Baby Diaper crimes.

She headed out of the area in the parking lot where the most recent murder had been committed. Her mind was reeling with all the information she'd been privy to just by being there to photograph the crime. The photos she took went through her mind, and she tried to remember each detail, as she walked.

"Patricia, wait up," a familiar voice interrupted her innermost thought process, but didn't quite make it all the way in.

She kept walking as if in a trance. The voice had interrupted on some level, but the words had not sunk into her brain. Fingers curled around her ribcage, and she jumped and screeched in an extremely undignified manner.

"Ticklish?" he teased, as she tried to pull herself together. It was Tony. His eyes looked wild and daring. He had a straight white grin that seemed to shout trouble warnings to her, behind blood red lips that seemed wet and dripping with secrets and depth. Her heart did the usual racing bit with an added spasm in her lower stomach. Though not altogether unpleasant, she didn't understand it. She had never reacted physically to anyone like this ever before.

"Tony," she gasped, pulling herself out of the maze of thought tormenting her brain.

"Wasn't that a rush?" he asked breathlessly with the grin never leaving his face. Did he mean being tickled? Obviously, it was. The screech alone revealed that. She was confused. Her mind took charge, and she realized he was referring to the murder scene.

She was glad that he had forgotten his previous question. Usually, that answer led to a few tortured minutes for her at the merciless tickling fingers of another. He was definitely referring to the crime scene. She could tell, though the fog in her brain tried to say differently.

"That's not quite the word I would use," she answered safely, no matter what he was talking about, as she began walking toward her dorm again.

"Come on. Who are you trying to kid? You wanted to be in the mix so bad you could taste it, and I saw your face when you got in. I know you thrived on being part of all that," he spoke in an accusatory tone, following her a little too closely.

She stopped to look him straight in the eye and protest vehemently, but found that she couldn't. The truth was that she had wanted to be part of it, and getting in, even accidentally, had proven to be an amazing experience. Digging deep into her soul, she also knew that she had thoroughly enjoyed it, even though she wished that the victims had not been people either she knew or had run across on campus, or even people at all.

"See, I knew it," he gushed, as if he could read her thoughts loud and clear. "Why don't we work together? I'll tell you everything I know, and you tell me everything you know," Tony offered before she could flinch from the truthfulness of his words. "If you don't work with me, I'll hold you down and tickle you until you tell me everything you know, anyway," he promised in a tormenting kind of tone.

Was he serious? Would he do that? She wasn't sure if it was a joke or not. She chose not to chance it. She didn't know if her poor confused brain could take his being that close for that long, never mind the tickling part. She eyed him in defeat. Not only would she have confessed within thirty seconds if he tickled her like that, but he had nailed her completely on the other points as well.

He was right, at least about this part of his opinion of her. She had a hunger for more, a thirst for learning and the drive to try to solve the case. She nodded her head, and they walked together, exchanging knowledge and information about what each had seen and heard at the scene.

She had hoped that DNA could be taken from the body, but he told her that the lab had found a piece of latex glove on the body. The perpetrator had not bathed her, but a baby wipes package without wipes had been found in a nearby trashcan. Someone wearing gloves had applied lotion and powdered her.

That shot down the hope of prints, but there could still be a strand of hair or some other unseen clue. Pat hoped that the victim had tried to fight back. If that were the case, DNA might be under her nails or somewhere on her body. A sense of disappointment overwhelmed her as Tony put all of those hopes to rest. The officers he had overheard talking had said that there was nothing substantial to go on.

"The wounds were different." Pat reiterated what she had seen first hand, as she photographed the body at the crime scene. "They think she was strangled, instead of drowned. There were bruises on her neck. The fingers had to be huge, though." Pat remembered them, as a shiver ran up her spine.

"Maybe the killer is escalating to satisfy his needs, or maybe it was a copy cat or something," Tony half said, half asked. Pat looked at him sharply. She had thought the same thing.

"You could be right," she said breathlessly, as if a light bulb had gone off in her head. "I have a friend at the police station. I'll mention that to him," she added. Her brain was in full swing, and her mind was reeling in thought process. This new victim might not have been a Baby Diaper Murder victim.

"Tony, can you get us into the morgue?" she asked directly. Since he wanted to work together, now was the time to share.

"No problem. Why?" he asked, raising his eyebrows above wild eyes. His lips became red and wet again, as if he were a wolf on the prowl about to devour its cornered prey.

She shook off the uneasy feeling for the greater good. To get what she needed, she would just have to put up with Tony's weirdness and the reactions she had to him. Pat sat forward and told him that she needed to examine the body herself. Though she knew that she only knew the absolute basics of forensic science to date, she hoped that her knowledge combined with his would help her.

CHAPTER TEN

I t was slightly past midnight when Tony led Pat into the morgue. It was empty of activity, except one sleeping security guard in a small closet-sized office with a small television set loudly, blasting highlights of the latest football game.

Pat could not help being chilled to the bone, as she followed Tony through the cement fortress. There were slabs, drawers, and tables full of bottles, tubes, burners, and utensils needed for this kind of work. The tables and slabs were stainless steel, and there were huge lights above two tables centered in the middle of the death abyss. Pat followed Tony into a smaller room. It was refrigerated, and there were huge drawers. He pulled one out. The sound of rolling thunder filled the room, and Pat wondered if they would be caught because of it.

Tony unzipped the black bag that held the body of the victim found in the van. The smell nearly knocked Pat out, as it wafted into the surrounding air.

"Imagine if it wasn't cold in here," Tony said, putting a hand over his nose and mouth.

She nodded and quickly looked over the body, which was bluish gray now. The lips were an eerie purple. Pat re-examined the marks on the neck. The fingers were pointed upward, as if he was holding her jaw too. She had apparently fought back for all she was worth.

The body was not bloated, as if the victim were drowned. Instead, it was clearly suffocation by strangulation, in Pat's opinion. She whispered as much to Tony, who acknowledged her findings and concurred with her diagnosis.

"What does the toe tag say?" Pat asked Tony and pointed to the foot.

Tony read it to her. "The girl's name is Joanne Lantana. She was twenty-two years old, five foot three, with dark hair and blue eyes. She weighed approximately 110 pounds." Tony looked up at her when he finished.

"Chart says she was a business major, wanted to run a restaurant, and was currently employed at The Little Lunch House." Pat added what she read.

"I know that place," Tony nodded, as he whispered.

"I want to find someone that knew her and ask him or her background questions," Pat spoke, as she continued scanning the chart for any other pertinent information.

They zipped up the bag, put the chart back on her chest, and closed the drawer slowly. Tony took her hand and retraced the same path they had taken in. Pat wondered if her heart was going to beat its way out of her chest.

"I'm going to The Little Lunch House tomorrow after classes. That's two girls too many associated with the diner. Do you want to join me?" Pat asked Tony, as they walked back toward her dorm.

"Yes, I'll meet you in the parking lot," he responded enthusiastically.

Her stomach enjoyed a slight convulsion at the mention of getting together with him the next day. She knew that he wanted to be a medical examiner. He had told her that when they met. She assumed that his enthusiasm was because of that. "The thrill of the ride," so to speak, but it still unnerved her a little bit.

She just wanted to solve the crime and avenge the death of someone she knew and liked, as well as put the other victims to rest in peace. Their families deserved that. At least that was what she told herself.

Tony was a maverick in the field, she guessed. Perhaps together, they would prove to be a great team. Pat grinned a little to herself. It always worked on television after all. She would be the straight-shooting, focused, serious one, and Tony would be the nut who pushed her to the brink of insanity while forcing her into the exact position she needed to be in to solve the crime. She tried to conceal her grin from Tony, but the thought wouldn't go away.

She said good night to Tony and was back inside her dorm room in a flash. She logged on her computer, used her password to get in her secret files, and went into the file holding her journal. The file wasn't marked clearly. She had labeled it as her holiday shopping list. No one would look there for her journal. If they got into it by mistake somehow, they would find a shopping list just as it was labeled. The journal started on the third page.

Pat gave herself a mental good job wink, as the file opened at her command. She typed in the latest series of events concerning the Baby Diaper Murder case. She told herself silently that she could refer to it later when she needed to write the paper for psychology.

Pat logged off with a yawn and climbed into bed for the night. Nightmarish dreams and clouded thoughts kept her tossing and turning in her bed throughout the night. She needed to talk to someone who knew Joanne—someone who knew her habits, her personality type, and background information. She hoped to shed a little more light on the death of the young woman. It wasn't just a project anymore. It was becoming a vendetta.

Try as she would, she could not stop the swirl of faces in her mind or rid herself of the foul stench of death seeming to cling to her even now. She thought of LuAnn and the girl in the van. She went over the photos in her mind and her conversations with Cameron.

She found herself dwelling on Cameron. She felt a simplistic attraction to him. The fit with her family could be amazing. He was kind, smart, and so good looking. He was everything that they had dreamed of in a man suitable for her. She didn't cringe at the idea, either, which made it worth looking into a little deeper.

He was a dream come true for any girl that she knew, that was for sure. She felt melancholy thinking of that. She smiled, as the thought infiltrated her brain farther. She could see them together, forming a future, a couple for better or worse 'til death did them part. She hugged herself and tried to stop her mind there. Her brain was having no part of any kind of pause.

Then, there was Tony. He appeared wild and crazy one minute, then quiet and sensitive the next. He could go places she never could. Not just that, though—he took her with him at will. He revved up her proverbial motor without so much as blinking an eye. He was like forbidden fruit—so seemingly dangerous that it was sexy.

Whenever he came within three feet of her, her heart reeled with excitement. When he touched her, he caused massive emotional explosions within her. The attraction to him was unlike anything she had ever felt before. He was a bad boy in every sense of the word, and not someone she'd likely bring home to meet her parents.

Still, just thinking about him caused a spasm in her lower stomach. It wasn't like her to react instantly animalistic or primal with any male. She chalked it up to some kind of human chemical unbalance and warned herself to proceed with caution. Her lower stomach did not listen to the sound advice and contracted pleasantly again.

Her mind drifted to Annie and Candy. They were not prepared to deal with anything beyond their own shallow eyesight, yet they were right in the throes of the situation. She thought of Sunny. She'd changed so much recently. She seemed almost cleansed in a way. Her demeanor seemed more at peace, yet still engulfed in sadness.

Morning finally arrived. Pat got ready and rushed off to her first class. She'd barely slept. She tried to focus. Though she didn't pay much attention in class, she did work. She put a list together of things she wanted to know about the latest murder victim. Though not an expert in any sense, she wanted to see if she could determine if this was an actual Baby Diaper Murder or a copycat's act.

She donned her white lab coat to get through her last class of the day. She looked at blood samples through a microscope and learned to determine blood type and Rh factors. That was really child's play for her, but not so for everyone else, so she had to muddle through it, which was fine with her. Her mind was elsewhere, anyway.

She was peering into the lens of a microscope and trying to explain what she was doing to teach her very green lab partner, when she felt fingers curl around her waist. She jumped in a reaction to the ticklish sensation, and her lab partner grabbed the microscope before it crashed on to the laboratory floor.

Her lab partner was grinning and had a soft red blush to her cheeks. Tony stood beside her lab partner. His eyes danced with pleasure at her disheveled expense. He had that same grin surrounded by wet red lips. She could no longer focus.

Her heart and stomach did a little dance in reaction to his entrance. It took a moment to catch her breath. Why did he keep doing that? And for heaven's sake, how had he found out this minor flaw in her character? It wasn't as if she wore a sign that read, "Poke here."

"Are you nearly ready to go?" he whispered, breaking the silence.

"After class; what are you doing here?" she asked in disbelief of his moxie.

"Tormenting you," he answered with a shrug.

He was succeeding in more ways than he knew. She put a hand on her stomach to stop the inevitable spasm. He grinned, seemingly at her expense. She pretended not to notice or to be doing anything unusual, though not very successfully.

His lips were still that intense shade of wet red, and his dark eyes lit up with sparkles. Her stomach did another pleasant flip-flop, much to her great dismay, and she was happy that he couldn't read her mind. She not only lost control of herself; she had no idea of why she'd lost control in the first place.

Tony sat on the stool next to her while she tried valiantly to explain the concepts of typing blood to her partner. He was too close. She could feel him breathing on her neck, as she studied the drop of blood on the glass slide. It was a wash. She couldn't work with her body reacting to him the way it was. He was making her crazy without even trying. He made her feel completely, inexplicably wanton.

The professor gave the word to clean up the area and dismissed the class. She was thankful. Now, she could get back to the business of solving the crime, and her body would relinquish its hold on her to her brain with any luck. She was amazed at herself, though she spoke not a word of it. It was unlike her to be this way. She took a deep breath and followed Tony out of the classroom.

"I thought you were going to meet me at The Little Lunch House or in the parking lot there," she said more than asked, as they walked out of the building.

"I thought it would be more fun to go together," he grinned, as he responded. Somehow, she knew that he knew that he was right.

They discussed questions that they wanted to ask if they found anyone who wanted to talk to them about Joanne Lantana, the dead business major found in the van. Pat couldn't help being sad for her. What an awful way to go. Joanne had to have known for at least several minutes that the end was eminent. It just wasn't right. Pat was determined to stop this guy, no matter what it took.

That moment turned into one that was less than credible when they arrived at The Little Lunch House. The police were already there questioning servers, the cook, and the owner. Pat found herself scanning the area for Cameron and feeling disappointed when he wasn't there. She slid into a booth with Tony and took in the atmosphere of the tiny diner.

Behind the yellow Formica counter was a stainless steel wall. The wall had a shelf. Behind the shelf was the cooking area. In front of the counter, were four pronged stools covered with brown vinyl and held together by big round gold studs. Small booths lined the windows across from the counter where she and Tony sat. They were also lined with brown vinyl and studded like the stools. It was fairly cheap and cheesy but apparently did the job.

They both knew that they were going to get nowhere fast, so they slid into a booth and decided to listen without discussing it with each other. It was as if moving in sync came instinctively just for the moment. Pat only wished that she could keep her heart from reeling foolishly over this guy—

perhaps if he didn't touch her—but it was not as if she had control of that.

He wasn't her type, not even close. Her parents would completely disapprove; she was sure of it. Yet she felt such primal attraction to him. It was driving her crazy, but she had to put it aside for the greater good, no matter how hard it was.

The server came over, and they ordered burgers, fries, and Cokes. She tried to smile and be pleasant, but both Tony and Pat could see that she was completely on edge. Pat wondered if Joanne had been a friend of hers and said as much in a hushed voice, taking note that the poor woman was over by the chef placing their order. It would explain the level of nerves the server seemed to be experiencing. They continued analyzing the situation around them as inconspicuously as possible.

"Do you think it's a possibility that all the victims ate here at one time or another, and that's how the killer chose them?" Tony asked.

"That's a good theory. I wonder if the police are thinking the same thing. Apart from all going to the same college, the victims seem to have next to nothing in common," Pat whispered conspiratorially back.

It was certainly something more to go on than they had before. She wondered if she should mention it to Cameron. She scanned the area for him again, but he wasn't at the diner. She tried hard to listen, as the police questioned employee after employee, coming up empty with each one.

"You know, I thought the same thing," a strange voice said in a low tone. Pat looked around for where the voice had come from. She didn't see anyone. She looked at Tony with questioning eyes. Had he said that?

"What did you say?" Pat asked.

"I think that this could be where the victims ate," the voice said again.

"What?" Pat asked, looking from side to side for a hint of who was speaking. It didn't sound like Tony.

"Where are you?" Pat asked, keeping her voice low.

"Behind you in the next booth," the voice answered.

"Come and visit," Pat offered, sliding into the booth, creating a space for the unknown speaker to sit in and raising her eyebrows at Tony. He grinned.

"If I didn't know better, I'd think that was some kind of an offer," Tony whispered.

Pat felt her face flush, as a young girl slid into the booth next to her in the seat. She didn't acknowledge Tony's insinuation, but her body reacted pretty strongly even to the suggestion. He was literally driving her crazy. She had to work to focus on the situation.

"What makes you think that all the victims might have eaten here?" Pat asked her quietly.

The server came and delivered the meals, laid the check down, and wandered off before the girl could answer the question.

"I think that I might have been a victim," she whispered. Tony rolled his eyes as if to say that clearly this sweet young thing was a nut, without using the words.

"What on earth makes you think you were a victim? Are you dead?" Tony asked sarcastically. He hadn't even tried to quiet his tone. The young girl went completely white.

"Never mind," she said with a raspy voice, as her eyes filled with tears. She began to slide back out of the booth.

"No, wait," Pat said, touching her arm and glaring at Tony. She just knew that the girl needed to say something, although she had no idea what or why. Even if what she was going to say was completely unrelated to the case, they owed it to LuAnn and all the rest of the victims to listen.

This poor girl might have been a victim of some other crime if not the one they were investigating. Pat felt that it needed further inquiry to find out. She wasn't ready to dismiss any lead, no matter how small or outrageous it might seem now.

"What's your name?" Pat asked gently in the most coaxing voice she could come up with on short notice.

"My name is Tia Macalusa. My friend's call me Mac. I eat here all the time," she said with her voice harsh and breaking off at the last sentence, while she looked at Tony with daggers coming from her eyes.

Mac looked to be about sixteen. She was about four foot eleven and about ninety-five pounds soaking wet. She had a thick dark mane of dark brown shoulder-length hair that was just short of black. Her eyes were big, blue, and shaped like almonds. The blue was like a crystal marble and lined with a thick black line. Her lashes were long, black, and luxurious. Any female would dream of aspiring to the beauty that this young girl obviously came into naturally.

"Mac, why do you think that you were a victim of the Baby Diaper Murderer?" Pat asked her gently. She figured that it was much more sensible to let her explain than to jump to conclusions. Tony seemed to understand instinctively what she was doing. He sat back and let Pat handle it, knowing he had already made a mistake in handling the young girl's story.

"I left here the other day, and I felt as if someone was following me. My head felt funny, and I got crazy dizzy. It was getting dark, and then someone grabbed me in the parking lot. I woke up in a hotel room. I was lying on a bed. My head was spinning, but I don't drink. It was… I don't know…." Mac looked for a word to describe her emotion. "Really frightening," Mac finished, still unsatisfied with her description.

"What then?" Pat asked, prompting her to continue.

"I heard a waterfall, or what I thought was a waterfall. I realized that I had no clothes on. It was so dark. It felt as if I was coming off drugs or something. Someone kept talking to me," Mac explained, as tears fell on to her cheeks, and she brushed them away. Even Tony was listening now. The waterfall got him.

"The murderer came and picked me up. He was carrying me into the bathroom. The waterfall was a tub faucet," Mac said.

"How did you escape?" Tony asked, hanging on her every word.

"I heard Sensei's voice. He instructed me, and I did what he said," she answered.

"Who is Sensei?" Pat asked, confused.

"I'm a black belt. I've studied karate since I was small. Sensei wasn't with me, but I remembered his instructions on self-defense so well, and I was so drugged up that I just followed them," she said, as if she understood that what she was saying sounded fabricated.

"How exactly did you get away?" Tony stressed his words, totally intrigued by what she was saying.

"I hit him in the nose. I'm sure it wasn't a proper palm heel, but I'm sure that I hit him," she said, holding her hand up to demonstrate the karate maneuver she had effectively used. Her hand looked as if she were telling someone to stop with

81

her palm facing away from her, only her fingers tilted back toward her body. The meat by the bottom of her thumb was a light blue bruised color.

"And then what happened?" Tony asked with wide eyes.

"He dropped me. I staggered to the door, and he grabbed me. I fell," she said, wiping her tears away again. She took a deep breath, composed herself, and continued. "I remember twirling and whirling and fighting. I'm good at grappling when I'm on the mat. Then, I got out the door, somehow. I ran and ran," she explained.

Pat and Tony had both heard the term grappling and knew that it was wrestling, except that the pin is on the stomach instead of the back, allowing the victim to render the opponent helpless.

"I was running naked on a road. I didn't know where I was, and Joanne picked me up in the street. She took me home in her van, and the next day I found out that she was dead."

"Wow," Pat said, gushing with awe.

"Can you remember anything else?" Tony asked.

"His face was covered with something. I think that the killer had very thick clothes on. He was as big as Frankenstein. He had huge feet," Mac replied.

"He had on thick clothes? What do you mean? Like he was cold?" Pat asked, trying to sort out the facts.

"I guess so. They were very soft. It was all kind of a blur," Mac said, trying to remember.

"So, he was very big and wore thick, soft clothing, with big feet. At least that's something," Pat summed up the new details.

"But they were inside, and he was running water," Tony questioned the story a bit.

"It doesn't make sense," he said, confused.

"Well, I was pretty drugged up, but I gave it to you as I remember it," Mac said apologetically.

"These are the bruises from his feet," she said, lifting her shirt and showing black and purple ribs.

"My knees are black; my elbows are rug burned like some other parts of my body; and my hand is bruised where it met with his face. I'm sure that I hit him." She tried to show them the parts not designated as private by society, without calling too much attention to herself.

"I definitely believe you," Tony said, and Pat agreed.

"I know it's farfetched, but I want to catch this jerk. This is where he must have drugged me," she said, as though she was unsure they believed her story.

"He's murdering women, remember. None of it makes sense," Pat reassured her.

"It doesn't make sense yet," Tony added, raising his eyebrows and finishing her train of thought.

"Do you attend classes at the college?" Pat asked, thinking that she was too young.

"No, but my sister does. I go to see her all the time. Does that mean anything?" Mac asked.

She, too, had every reason to want to solve the Baby Diaper Murder case, Pat and Tony both completely understood. An alliance began at that exact moment. No one spoke the words, but all three parties knew what the outcome of the conversation had to be. They were destined to join forces whether they wanted to or not. Three heads were better than two were.

"So, now, we have two new details and are more confused than ever," Pat said.

Tony nodded. Before Mac, the only linking piece of information was that they all attended the same college. Now, the information took a detour, but it was possible the killer thought she attended the college too. She had clearly said that she was at the college all the time and frequented The Little Lunch House, which serviced the college students as their primary source of customers. But the question remained—What if the killer did know about the diner? What then was connecting the victims? How were they picked?

Cameron Scott joined his fellow officers moments later, and Pat seriously entertained the notion of telling him what Mac had said. She decided against it, as he took grief for being late from his friends. They were calling him "promptness impaired," while laughing at his expense. Pat chose to ignore it and him for the time being. Focusing on Mac had her full attention, anyway. She wanted to see if Mac could remember any other details.

P at had separated from Mac and Tony to get back to the dorm and write down what she knew in her journal. Sunny was sitting on the wall of the fountain. It was obvious that she'd been crying. That being an extremely unusual sight, Pat naturally found herself heading directly toward her to see if she could help. Sunny was the next best thing she had to family here at the college, and she felt very close to her.

As she drew closer, the scene looked much worse. Sunny was actually sobbing. It looked so pathetic and so sad that Pat felt her heart reeling just from the sight. She sat down next to Sunny, reached up, and put an arm around her massive shoulders.

"What on earth is wrong?" Pat asked, as gently as her voice would allow.

"Tiffany-Crystal... she... I..." Sunny sobbed uncontrollably.

She seemed unable to control herself, as her huge body convulsed involuntarily. Pat didn't know what to do, so she held her and waited until Sunny could speak. She thought that Sunny's mother had died but waited for Sunny to tell her.

When she finally gained control of herself enough to tell Pat what was going on, Pat was floored by the news. Sunny's mother hadn't died. The problem was just the opposite. New life had occurred.

85

Tiffany-Crystal had just given birth to a beautiful bouncing baby boy. He weighed in at a petite five pounds and three ounces and was eighteen inches long. Her parents had named the baby Ralph, Jr. They had written to Sunny and sent pictures. He was the boy they had always dreamed of. Sunny had not even been told that Tiffany-Crystal was expecting.

She was devastated and unequipped to handle this new set of cards dealt her by the people she had fought to be loved and accepted by for her entire existence. Pat had never felt sorrier for anyone or been privy to a more disgusting show of parenting skills than those of Ralph, Sr. and Tiffany-Crystal. How could they treat their child like that?

When Sunny seemed calm enough, Pat left, instructing her to go back to her dorm and get some rest. It frayed her last nerve to think about Sunny's parents. There was really nothing more that she could do for her friend than worry. She was an older sister now, for better or worse until death did them part.

It was so sad. People need a license to drive a car, but anyone could bring a poor unsuspecting baby into the world. Pat felt like writing to the President or her congressional representative or someone to suggest that they bring forth a bill in Congress making it mandatory for people to pass a test before being allowed to procreate. Of course, she knew that the thought was ridiculous, but it would sure beat the feeling of helplessness she was dealing with on behalf of her friend at the moment.

A sense of defeat seemed to overcome Pat, as she sat down at her computer. Though she knew that her own feelings on the subject were nothing next to the enormity in the way Sunny was forced to live them, it just seemed so hopeless sometimes. She typed the new information halfheartedly into her journal and then lay down on her bed. She drifted into a tormented sleep full of nightmares about monsters and murders and people screaming.

One scream would not stop, no matter how much she tossed and turned. With slow recognition, she was brought out of the dream world and back into reality where, much to her instant shock, the screams were real.

She fought to untangle the covers and fell out of bed in a mad dash to help whoever was screaming in the hallway. She scrambled to her feet and stumbled toward the door, realizing that she was wearing only her underwear. Her eyes felt heavy, and her cheeks felt thick, as she fought to scan the area for her pants.

Pat pulled a skirt from her hamper and zipped it up, as she hurried to the door. The screams had turned to pleading sobs for help. Just outside her door, the hallway was quickly filling with people who had come to the rescue of the unknown screamer. She pushed her way through the crowd, as she felt a lump of glue form in her throat. Please let the screaming be caused by a mouse or something like that—anything but another murder, she prayed silently.

She knew that her prayers had gone unanswered when she got two doors down in the same hallway as her own dorm room.

"Somebody call the police. Don't touch anything. Everyone needs to stand back." Pat heard herself shouting orders with a voice that she recognized as her mother's outside voice. The voice meant, "If you think I'm kidding, try me."

She put her arms around the sobbing girl, while the girl cried into her shoulder. Her name was Jette Simon. Jette had hair so black that the highlights were natural blue. She was of Asian decent. She had smooth blemish-free, olive skin; she was just a smidgen above being too thin and normally lovely to look at. Now, however, she was an overwrought heap of human flesh, convulsing her body involuntarily with each sob. Her hair was loose and tangled, and she didn't care a bit about it.

Pat soothed her as best she could, which was impossible given the circumstances. Jette had come home and found her friend Andrea dead on the bed. Through tears of anguish, she told Pat that her regular roommate, Janice, and she were file clerks in the headquarters of an appliance parts chain in town. Janice was working the night shift and had invited Andrea to stay over for the night.

Andrea commuted to work, and apparently, it was a far drive. She had stayed over often, and normally, it didn't present a problem. Jette choked on the last word and crumpled against Pat, who immediately helped her to a chair.

Pat could hear police sirens in the distance getting louder and louder, as the officers of the law sped to the scene of the crime. She knew that it would only be a matter of moments before they arrived and began the tedious evidence-gathering search that would hopefully catch this murdering lunatic.

"Somebody, get her some water." Tony's voice found its way through the still assembling crowd before his body did.

Pat looked up. With her eyes, she motioned to the bed. Tony nodded slightly. There was no question that Andrea had been another victim of the Baby Diaper Murderer. Her body was laid on its side; her thumb was in her mouth; her diaper was what looked to be a white long-sleeved blouse; and pillows were positioned so that she was "safe." Her eyes were closed to appear that she was sleeping peacefully. She didn't smell too bad yet, which made Pat think that the murder was recent. She had been bathed, lotioned, and powdered just as the other victims.

The room filled up quickly. Cameron and his partner Tom were among the first officials on the scene. The photographer wasn't far behind. Pat held Jette while she retold the story about how Andrea had ended up in her dorm room dead. Cameron wrote everything down, as she spoke.

Andrea Romano, or Andi, as all her friends called her, was a file clerk at the appliance store in town. She had been too tired to drive home and Janice had given her the key to the room so that she could sleep for a while because they had stayed out very late the night before the alleged murder. Jette had been out late with some friends and had come home to take a shower and go to bed. She had come into the room and found Andi dead. She remembered screaming loudly for a long time.

Cameron acknowledged the information, and he was thanking her when the photographer fell against him. He dropped his pad and lowered the photographer to the ground gently. The camera had not fallen. The photographer had held it steadfast, as he passed out. He did spill his water on the floor, which contaminated that part of the crime scene.

"Now, what'll we do?" One official working the scene asked.

"The photographer's assistant is right over here with me," Cameron said, looking Pat straight in the eye and giving a wink. She stifled a grin, and a rosy hue formed on her cheeks. Cameron was very pleased to see that she had dimples on each side of her smile and found it both cute and entrancing.

Without a word, Pat picked up the Hasselblad, walked over to the bed, and photographed everything the men in charge told her to and took several that she thought they might need to see. Cameron had gotten her a way in. This time, the photographer would have to give her credit.

Perhaps she could use that to persuade him to let her assist all the time until the murderer was caught. She didn't want any pay. She just wanted to catch the perpetrator who had killed her friend LuAnn among the many others and attacked her new friend Mac. This guy needed to be put away for good. The experience in her field and the psychology paper were also a good bonus, but she'd have gladly given all that up to have LuAnn back alive and well. She would like to have them all back alive and well.

Tony grinned at her from across the room, and she felt her heart skip a beat and then jump around a little. She moved her eyes out of his lock and went to give the photographer back his camera.

"I guess I have a new assistant," he said in a low voice and then held his head as if it were about to split open.

"Pat Farmer," she reminded him softly. He nodded. "Please call me if there is a next time. One victim was a friend of mine," she mentioned in a prodding tone. He nodded again. His eyes told volumes, and they said clearly that he now understood her persistence and interest in being involved in such a heinous crime such as serial murder. They also said that he'd call her.

The Dean cancelled classes the next day, much to Pat's agreement. She was so tired that she could barely function. After being sure that every second of every minute she had witnessed at the crime scene was recorded in her journal, she fell onto her bed spread eagle and stared at the ceiling until sleep finally overcame her.

She woke up to the sounds of bumping and thumping in the hallway. When she peered out, she saw Jette and two older people she assumed were Jette's parents. Another young adult, slightly younger than Jette, was carrying her belongings out into the hallway and complaining in another language. Although Pat didn't speak the language he was using, she definitely understood the tone. He was obviously unhappy about hauling all her things out of the dorm on such short notice. He didn't understand.

"Are you leaving, Jette?" Pat called out into the hall so that she could hear. When she turned toward Pat, she looked like a complete stranger. Jette's eyes were red and nearly swollen shut. The pallor to her face was frightening, and she was ever so slightly hunched over in emotional pain.

Trauma dripped from her eyes, and she nodded. Pat went into the hallway and picked up two suitcases. She followed the younger male out to the car and then came back for another load. Jette's family thanked her profusely. They just wanted their little girl to come home and be safe. They were pulling her from college, and she didn't seem to mind.

Pat noticed many students pulling out after that. Packed up cars, vans, and trucks left the campus for nearly the rest of the week. The campus seemed much emptier than it had in the past few months. It made her feel a bit forlorn.

CHAPTER TWELVE

Pat's phone rang, interrupting the latest entry in her journal. Without so much as a glance at who might be calling, she picked up the line.

"Hello," she said distractedly.

"Hello, yourself," a familiar voice said into her ear. Chills ran up her spine. She hadn't expected the call. It was Cameron, and he instantly had her full attention. She remained calm and demure as a purposeful act.

"How on earth did you get my number?" she asked innocently, knowing that she'd given it to him at the police station after Jacqueline had been murdered. She was glad to hear from him. It excited her, and she had to fight to maintain composure. She just couldn't believe that he'd called her.

"I was wondering if you'd like to get together," he asked with confidence. She fell backward on her bed. She tried not to accept too quickly, but failed miserably.

"Yes. I mean… to talk about the case or what?" she stammered. He chuckled on the other end of the line, and she wanted to kick herself for sounding like a thrilled adolescent, although he didn't seem to mind.

"Well, we can talk about the case if you choose, but I'd rather just go out and grab a soda, maybe listen to some good music. I'm pretty sick of murder," he explained. She understood. Amid all the mayhem and craziness, police officers still needed to have some sort of life. She wouldn't mind a little normal time herself, now that he'd mentioned it.

"That would be great," she gushed without trying to.

A date! He was asking her out on a date. She said a silent thank you toward heaven. They agreed to meet at the Sound Rave, which was a non-alcoholic music club on the far south side of the college campus. Pat couldn't have been more thrilled. She hung up the phone and immediately began going through her closet for something to wear.

She chose a pair of black jeans with a black tube top and threw a fuchsia jacket over it. She piled her hair on top of her head and let little wispy curls sneak out in exactly the right places, making her look sophisticated, a bit older in her opinion, and immensely attractive. Two gold necklaces with a bracelet and matching earrings left her ready and looking amazing. This wasn't just any guy. This was Cameron Scott, officer of the law, and a bit older than she was.

She wanted to present herself as a fitting date for someone like him. One last look in the mirror told her that she had succeeded in that task, and she grabbed her purse and was off to meet him at the Sound Rave. In her mind, she, too, thought that a little dancing, relaxing, and a little socializing would do them each some good. Lord knows, they were up to their ears in the trauma bestowed on the college by the Baby Diaper Murderer.

Pat practically ran across the campus. Her heart throbbed in anticipation. Cameron Scott was the bomb! He was someone she could introduce to her parents. He was indeed the marrying kind that every woman hoped for—handsome, debonair, stable, and working. She hoped that he thought as much of her as she did of him.

Suddenly, Pat had a strange feeling that someone was watching her. She thought she heard footsteps nearby, but turned and saw no one. It got worse, and she felt as if she were being stalked and then chased. Sweat formed on her upper lip, and then she broke out into a full run until she couldn't run anymore. She stopped to suck in gulps of air and pull herself together before Cameron spotted her psychotic behavior. It was all the murders. She was too close to them these days. They had her spooked. She couldn't shake off the feeling, as she approached her destination.

The music from the Sound Rave fell on her ears minutes before she had a visual of the club. As she rounded the bend of patio sidewalk, stragglers and small groups of people were milling about, waiting for friends, and talking to each other. There was laughter. Pat hadn't heard that sound in a while and immediately realized just how much she had missed it. She scanned the area for any sign of Cameron.

The building looked like most of the other buildings on the campus. It had a great big brownstone front with orange slate roofing. The walks that weren't patio cement were made of cobblestone and had been there since the days of the horse and buggy, or so she had been told. White pillars held up a roof with no walls, creating the entrance into the Sound Rave. It was clearly newer and more modern than the rest of the building. Red velvet ropes and silver holders roped it off along the path. It looked like the place to be if she wanted to have some fun, which she most definitely did. She continued to scan the area, as the crowd closer to the entrance thickened around her.

"Hello there," someone said, as he grabbed her elbow gently.

She whirled around and looked Cameron right in the eye. He smiled broadly, and his cheeks seemed to turn a light shade of pink, which dazzled her momentarily, until she found herself smiling back. She had known instantly that it wasn't Tony. His entrance would've been one that startled her or made her yelp, causing the huge crowd to stare in her direction. Her stomach would've been keeping beat with the music already.

"Hello, yourself," she replied.

She felt so comfortable and so happy to be with Cameron. It was a wonderful feeling, and if that exact second would've been frozen in time, she wouldn't have minded one little bit. He escorted her into the club, and she was thrilled to be on his arm. Having full control of her reactions gave her a sense of empowerment, and she enjoyed it.

The inside of the club looked nothing like the outside. It was completely done up in modern lighting. It rocked with surround sound speakers and had two stages for live performers and three bars, even though they prided themselves on being an alcohol-free zone for young people to go and have fun. It was breathtaking.

Cameron found a table for them between one bar and one stage. He offered to go get her a soda, and she gratefully accepted. She watched, as he disappeared into the thick, swaying crowd. His movements were graceful and confident, which she admired so much in a person. She felt that she tended to be a little clumsy, on the shy, quiet side, and carried herself as such. Lately, she erred on the side of caution and carried herself any way she could to stay aware of what was going on around her.

"Pat," a familiar voice said, approaching her table.

Pat turned her head to see who was calling her. Against the music, it was very hard to know without seeing, but her body betrayed her. It was Tony. She was glad that he'd used his voice to get her attention, instead of the ten tickling fingers he seemed so fond of using on her. Her brain instantly fogged, and she grabbed a lock of her hair to twirl unconsciously. Her stomach did the involuntary flip-flop, and her heart began to race uncontrollably. Why did he have this effect on her? Why did her body become erratic and go awry whenever he was within fifty feet of her. It was unnerving. He hadn't even touched her. Should she be wishing that he would? What was wrong with her?

"Hi, Tony," she said, forcing herself to smile and pretending that she was completely normal.

"You look seriously outrageous," he said, getting too close to her, which obviously meant he liked what he saw. She felt his breath on her neck, as he talked directly into her ear. Goose bumps shot up her spine. Her lungs betrayed her too. She couldn't breathe properly. Why did he have to say that? Not that it was unpleasant—just bad timing. Perhaps next time he could show up when she was inhaling.

"Hey, Pat's here," another surprised voice said, walking up behind Tony. It was Mac. She put her hand on the small of Tony's back, as she got to the table.

Pat's entire body stopped cold. It was as if all the involuntary actions that had gone on only moments before ceased to be operational now. It was almost painful. She had to fight to suck it up.

"Mac, uh… hi, are you two together?" Pat found herself asking with someone else's voice.

Tony grinned with that wet redness forming on his lips. His eyes danced and sparkled and she had to look away, although she couldn't figure out why. He wasn't her type at all, not even close. So, why then, was his presence making her crazy? And why was his being with Mac so important? Why had her body just frozen solid like that? What was wrong with her?

"We met here," Mac answered innocently.

Pat wondered if the touch to Tony's back was just as innocent and then mentally slapped herself right across the face. It was none of her business what they did or did not do; what Mac felt for Tony or did not feel. She needed to get her thought process to turn another way. She couldn't believe the things happening in her mind. It was as if a volleyball game were going on in full force, using her emotional wellbeing as the ball. She knew that she was clearly out of bounds in her line of thinking.

"Come on, let's dance," Mac nagged sweetly and tugged at Tony's arm. They went off onto the dance floor directly centered in the middle of everything and were gone from sight within seconds. Pat suddenly felt lonely.

"Here's the soda. Boy, what a mob scene at the bar," Cameron said, placing the sodas on the table and sitting down across from her.

She tried to put the Tony questions out of her mind and thanked heaven that her body parts were all working in proper order again so that she could concentrate on Cameron. Part of her wondered why it was so easy to maintain control around Cameron and not Tony. She chalked it up to his being older.

She asked Cameron what brought him to the area to strike up a conversation and hopefully break the ice. He told her that he had come from a small town—the kind where everyone knew everyone else's business—and although he found himself missing that at times, he had traveled to the area to join the force and do something good with his life. He had used the word epic in the complete description. He wanted his life to have meaning. It only seemed fitting that he should do that, considering his background, in his opinion.

He had Pat's undivided attention, except for a wayward glance or two toward the dance floor to see if she could spot Tony and Mac. The glances were unsuccessful and went unnoticed by Cameron as he spoke.

Cameron went on to tell her that his mother had been a nurse in the war. She had been stationed very close to the front lines. A bombing had occurred, and innocent civilians, many of them children, were hurt. At one point, the makeshift hospital was filled with children, and a troop of men from the other side marched in shooting. His mother had dove at the leader, managed to get his gun away from him, and held the perpetrators at gunpoint until they left without harming anyone.

After they left, one lone gunman stayed behind, and when she dropped her guard, he took aim with his weapon. He was going to shoot her in the back of the head and kill her. Cameron paused to take a sip of his drink just then.

"What happened? Is she okay?" Pat asked, completely engulfed in the story. Cameron nodded.

"She's fine. This happened before she even knew that my father existed," he responded.

He continued to unfold the amazing story for her, as she sat riveted to her chair. His mother had bent down to hug a frightened, crying child. His father was lying in a cot among the wounded but noticed the gunman taking aim. His firearm was at his side. He grabbed it with his broken hand, shot the man right in the heart, and saved her life.

"That's how they met. Cross my heart," Cameron said, crossing his heart and holding his hand up as if he were under oath. His father's broken hand had never healed correctly because of that incident but he had met Cameron's mother who eventually became his wife.

"Holy cow," was all Pat could think of to say at that particular moment.

"So, you see what I'm up against? I need to solve these murders just to live up to the family name. I need to make them proud." Cameron explained his position to Pat in half a joking manner and felt that she completely understood.

She was so taken with him that there weren't words to describe the emotion. She was so glad to have met him and so proud that he had confided all the things about his life and his hopes to her. She would hold them very dear.

"What would it take to be your hero?" Cameron asked, looking her directly in the eye and using a voice that was sultry and seductive. She felt caught off guard, but the answer came out easily, as if some unknown force had fed it to her at exactly the right moment in time.

"You can solve this case, and then you will have my unwavering devotion," Pat said, knowing that she had given the perfect answer. He nodded and smiled as if to reassure her that he would indeed meet her demand.

Tony and Mac walked over to them, completely winded from dancing, and interrupted the moment. Tony threw himself into a chair, and Mac sat down like a normal person. Pat did quick first name introductions, as her body became someone else's with a will of its own and fully betrayed her brain. Mac mentioned what a great place the Sound Rave was, and everyone agreed.

"Sunny," Pat said, surprised to see her there as well. "Sunny is one of my dearest friends. I love her, and we're very close. Just wait until you meet her," she said, giving Cameron the quick rundown of her friendship with Sunny.

Cameron didn't have time to answer before Sunny got to the table. Her eyes spoke volumes about being happy to see Pat. Sunny looked surprised too. She put her soda down on the table and asked Pat to watch it for a second because she wanted to go to the ladies' room. It was a hint for Pat to come along, and Pat knew that.

"I'll go with you," Pat offered, knowing that if she didn't go now, she'd have to go soon anyway, and that this was the perfect way. With the way things were going, her bladder might pop and betray her like the rest of her insides were. Vaguely, she wondered if it was a conspiracy—organs against brain—and which would win. She grinned to herself at her own neurotic joke and behavior, as she followed Sunny to the ladies' room so that they could talk.

Sunny seemed to be coming to terms with having a little brother, but the pain was still new, and her heart was sore. Her parents had not done the right thing by keeping her in the dark about the baby. Sunny had been worried that there was something wrong medically with Tiffany-Crystal for months.

She was clearly relieved that her mother was not ill, but the baby boy still had her reeling. He was healthy, as far as she knew, and truly, she was glad about that. She too had a volleyball game going on in her brain. Pat could identify with the symptoms, although the reasons for their respective matches were very different.

She confided her secret body attacks where Tony was concerned to Sunny after that. They grew closer than two friends had ever been in the short time they shared. They hugged each other tight before they left the bathroom, both knowing that the other would never betray her trust.

Cameron was at the table alone when the two girls got back to the table. Pat caught herself scanning the area for the duo once again and mentally kicked herself for it.

"Cameron, were you here before?" Sunny asked, suddenly stopping short.

"Yes, Sunny. How are you?" he asked in a cool tone.

"Can't complain," Sunny answered. Ice formed on her words. Pat was confused. Sunny's eyes instantly radiated sadness. She wasn't complaining, but there was no doubt in Pat's mind that Sunny was in agony over seeing Cameron.

"I heard that your mom had a baby," Cameron continued.

"Yes, she had a boy. Ralph junior," Sunny stammered.

Pat felt so sorry for her, but could say nothing without betraying what her friend had confided to her. It was torture to watch. Sunny drank a huge gulp of her soda. Her throat was drying out in the midst of emotional exposure.

"Wow, that's wonderful. They always wanted a boy, right?" he asked.

"Right," Sunny replied hoarsely.

Pat would've kicked him under the table if she could've found his leg, though she knew that he had no clue that he was hurting her and that she was devastated by the birth of her brother.

"Tell your parents that I send heartfelt congratulations," he said, closing the conversation much to Pat's great relief.

"Sure will," Sunny stuttered and held up her empty glass. "Got to go get a refill," she explained, as she walked away from the situation with grace, though her dignity was questionable.

Clearly, she and Cameron knew each other, or at least their families did. Pat chose not to approach the subject just then.

"What happened to Tony and Mac?" Pat asked Cameron.

"They went to dance. Speaking of which…" he motioned toward the dance floor with his eyes. She laughed and nodded. It was exactly what she wanted to do. It was getting much too tense at the table; that was for sure.

A short while later, they were back at the table, completely winded. Pat glanced at the bar and saw Sunny. She seemed to be feeling much better, as she laughed and chatted with a small group of people at the bar. Pat was relieved.

Sunny looked good that night, especially with the smile. She had on yellow gold pants, a white peasant shirt, and a paisley vest with gold woven through it, which sparkled in the bright lights. She'd definitely shed some pounds, although Pat could not be sure how many. It was nice to see her smiling.

"She's really something, huh?" Cameron interrupted her thoughts.

"Who do you mean—Sunny?" Pat asked, and then nodded in agreement.

"How do you know her?" Pat asked.

"Same small town, everyone knows everyone. She's an easy mark for any guy who needs an hour, you know?" he asked, hinting that Sunny was promiscuous.

"That just can't be. You must have the wrong girl," Pat said through a laugh.

"No, that's her," he corrected with a nod.

"Cameron, she's gay," Pat said with slight annoyance.

"Oh, really, did she tell you that cock-in-bull story?" Cameron asked with a sarcastic look on his face and pointed in the direction of the bar. Pat looked toward Sunny. It was an incredulous sight. Sunny, the self-professed lesbian was at the bar making out with a guy. Pat gasped and nearly choked on the air that had infiltrated her lungs. A coughing fit ensued, but her eyes remained fixed on her friend.

"Holy cow," she said again when she could finally speak.

"Don't believe anything you hear," Cameron instructed her, "and only half of what you see. Especially from her," he added.

She nodded dumbly. She was glad that she'd held her tongue. She knew that if another moment had passed, she would've given him the verbal lashing of his life, and it would've most likely ended any chance of a further relationship abruptly.

She watched Sunny continue to kiss the guy. Within seconds, Sunny was on his arm, and they were headed out the door. She noticed that Sunny tripped and staggered a little bit and was glad that her friend didn't fall, but she was astonished that she was indeed leaving the Sound Rave on the arm of a man.

There was also little left to the imagination as to where the two were headed. Cameron almost looked smug about it, which upset Pat a bit, though she said nothing. She was wrong about Sunny, even though she couldn't believe it. She didn't want to make it come between Cameron and her.

She scanned the area one more time for Tony and Mac to no avail. They, too, had left the club. Part of Pat wondered if they were locked away in each other's arms somewhere. Her heart sank a little at the thought. She was thrilled to be with Cameron, yet she just wanted to go back to her dorm and think about things. She couldn't figure out what was wrong, but supposed it had been the shock of her friends together and the added shock of seeing Sunny. It just didn't sit right with her.

Cameron was a perfect gentleman and walked her all the way back to her dorm. He took her key, opened the door for her, and then gave the key back. He kissed her gently on the lips, which made her tingle a little bit, and she rather liked it. Then, he was gone. No stars and rockets, but it was definitely nice enough. She lay on her bed thinking of the night's events. She was profoundly unwound, unfulfilled—not revved up. She didn't like that feeling at all. She felt like a lump of nothingness.

Was she jealous of Mac and Tony? Was she upset at Cameron for seeming so smug? Did someone she trusted and called her friend lie to her? Was she let down by the night's ending? Could they finally solve the Baby Diaper Murder case and be done with it forever? And if they could do that, then how could they do it? What was the answer? It was all too much. Pat fell into a hellish sleep full of demons and nightmares again. She wondered if it would ever end.

The telephone rang and startled her back into awareness. It was Cameron.

"I just wanted to say good night," he said in a whispery voice.

"I had a lovely time," she lied in reply.

"I'm glad. I did too," he said. "Would you like to do it again?" he asked.

"I'd love to," she answered. It wasn't a lie that time. He was clearly pleased on the other end of the line, and although no solid plans were made, they had made a commitment to at least one more date.

Pat hung up the phone, feeling much better. Cameron was great for her. She was thankful that he had called and deterred her awful mood. She was sure that she would sleep better now, and she was right.

CHAPTER THIRTEEN

Cameron phoned Pat again the next day and invited her to The Little Lunch House for coffee. He said that he'd had a wonderful time with her and had thought about her all night. She liked that he felt that about her and agreed to meet him for coffee. She wanted to give their relationship another chance. Things had just been "off" the night before; she was sure of it.

She pulled herself together, showered, and primped and was off. About halfway to The Little Lunch House, she had that same eerie feeling of being watched. She looked around, but saw no one. Goose bumps formed on the nape of her neck. She wasn't sure if it was the cool dampness of the morning air or the subdued fright now growing rapidly inside her.

Once again, she bolted for her destination. She wanted to get to Cameron, to safety. She hadn't told him about her previous experience because she hadn't wanted to ruin her first date with him, but she was definitely going to tell him this time.

When The Little Lunch House was within plain sight, she slowed down a bit. She sucked in air and looked around suspiciously. She knew that it was probably all in her head, a side effect of her life of late, but that didn't stop the fear from welling up inside her. She composed herself and walked through the entrance of the diner.

She slid into a booth, and Cameron came in moments behind her. He was carrying a small bouquet of handpicked flowers. Her heart melted at the sight of him.

"The Horticulture Department might be angry when they discover the missing flowers, but I thought you'd like these," he said, handing her the flowers and sliding into the seat across from hers.

She laughed and smelled the sweet aroma of the little bouquet. She didn't know anything about flowers other than they were pretty, and they smelled nice. She only hoped that these weren't some important hybrid experiment the horticulture department was working on to save humanity or something. She chose not to say that to Cameron and thanked him instead.

They both ordered coffee and muffins. She ordered blueberry; he ordered bran. If she'd known him a little better, she might have teased him about the bran, but since they were new at the dating game, she chose not to go there. Instead, she mentioned that she'd had a great time and had slept better after he'd phoned.

"Were you having trouble sleeping before I called? Was there something wrong?" he asked picking right up on her mistake. She gave herself a mental slap on the head. She hadn't wanted to say it like that.

"Well, I didn't tell you last night." She decided to mention the "imaginary" real life threat of the stalker. She explained that she hadn't wanted to worry him with her vivid imagination and that she was sure all the things going on at the college these days had just spooked her. She wanted him to know that she was trying not to overreact.

She wondered if she should mention that the same thing had happened this morning. He was an officer of the law after all. Wasn't he someone she really should tell? In a split second, she divulged the information. He sat staring at her as if in a trance.

"You need to be more careful. The murderer is still out there. I don't want you to get hurt," he cautioned her.

He sounded like her father, and it made her listen. Apparently, he did not think that she was overreacting; he thought the opposite. He reached over the table and took her hands gently. His hands were warm. His eyes were sincere, and his voice was protective. His eyes bore a hole through her as if to stress the point. She nodded.

"I really care about you. I know it's too soon," he said, averting his eyes to the table.

She knew that the circumstances they were treading through were playing an integral part of turning their possible relationship into a probable mess if someone didn't say something.

"I care about you too," she said genuinely and softly.

He looked up and into her eyes, and she felt warmth radiate from him. The server came over with their order, interrupting the special moment, and she was gone in a fatal flash with the damage done.

"How long have you known Sunny?" Cameron asked her, as they ate and spoke of family, friends, and college life.

"I drove her in on our first day. We started together," Pat replied.

"I had no idea that she went to this college. Just watch out around her, will you?" he asked and took another sip of his coffee.

"Why? She's harmless," Pat questioned him in a confused manner.

"To be honest, if I'd have known that she was here, I'd have looked closer at her for the murders," he confided in a low voice. He ran over his new theory quickly for her. "Listen to it from the investigation angle—woman completely unloved due to gender whose parents give birth to a little boy. She's definitely built like a man, so the strength is there. She lies about being gay. You do the math," he whispered. It didn't add up the same way for Pat.

"I don't think she's a murderer," Pat answered in defense of her friend.

"Yeah, and she's not gay, either," he said sternly, reminding Pat of the apparent lie Sunny had told everyone and how he believed she had too easily fallen prey to it.

Pat sipped her coffee. Part of her felt anger at Cameron, but she squashed it into her stomach. The other part of her knew that Sunny had indeed been devastated at the birth of Ralph Junior. She assumed that Cameron had guessed that by reading her reactions, as they spoke the night before. He was trained to do that.

She knew about the relationship Sunny had had with her parents because she was a girl, and not the prettiest girl at that. She had indeed been an eyewitness to Sunny's close encounter with the man at the bar. These thoughts wound through the crevices of her brain like a worm sucking information a little bit at a time from a computer. It sent a shiver up her spine. Still, all those things were far from murdering people.

"You okay?" Cameron asked her, as he noticed her body react to the involuntary shiver.

"Fine, I'll be careful," she assured him. He nodded. She could almost see his brain working the details of the new theory. He was wrong. She knew it in her deepest of depths. Sunny was troubled, but a murderer? No way.

Cameron had to get to work, and Pat had to get to her first class, so they parted ways at the door of The Little Lunch House. Cameron gave her his best heartwarming smile just before he kissed her gently on the lips. The kiss was sweet and warm. She tried to feign affection. She had a stomachache for some reason. She couldn't feel affection over it. Should she have to do that with someone she was supposed to care about more than a friend?

Signals went into her brain. The kiss and the time spent with Cameron were nice, but why wasn't she filled with that euphoric feeling she'd heard so much about? She smiled back at him, as he turned his back to her and walked away. She watched his long legs stride and his long lanky body gracefully go along for the ride.

The thought of Sunny being a suspect for murder bothered her a lot, as she walked across campus toward her class. She had to find the real murderer. It wasn't Sunny. Cameron was clearly barking up the wrong tree. She just hoped that he had not mentioned it to any of his superiors.

She sat in class listening to the professor lecture when she heard sirens in the distance. They were approaching the college rapidly, and all the students' nerves frayed on cue. There was no question. There must have been another murder committed on the premises.

Pat scooped up her books milliseconds before the professor dismissed them, anyway, and headed for the crowd forming several buildings away. She put her books down on a bench just outside the building, enabling her to get to the scene faster.

The police were putting the yellow tape around the scene when she got there and refused to allow her access to the sight. The photographer looked over, and their eyes met.

"Let her in. She's with me," he said, pointing to her.

"Oh, I'm sorry, miss. I didn't know," the officer holding the crowd at bay explained.

"No problem, I completely understand," Pat answered professionally, as he stepped aside.

"Thanks," she said to the photographer.

"Thank you. You're doing a great job," he assured her with an approving nod.

"Are you not well?" Pat asked in a whisper.

"I'm not sure. I've been having dizzy spells, but only at the Baby Diaper crime scenes.

Maybe it's finally getting to me after all these years," he said, quietly shaking his head. She patted his shoulder.

"You're secret is safe with me," she reassured him.

He smiled. He looked weary, and sweat was gathering on his semi-bald head. He didn't say another word. He took another swig of his water and handed her the camera. She knew without words that he was telling her that he was sick. It was happening again.

Cameron and his partner Tom were questioning people. A young girl was wrapped up in a blanket. She had been crying. Mascara ran down her cheeks, and her hair was completely mussed. She accepted a cup of tea from another officer working the scene. Her name was Kathy Seeley. She was in her second year of college.

She had gone to breakfast that morning with her roommate Pauline. After that, she'd gone to class. Pauline didn't have an early class that day, so she was going back to the dorm to study for an upcoming exam. She was studying library science and worked part time in the town library. Kathy had realized that she'd forgotten a book and needed to go back to their room to get it. She'd found Pauline dead when she got there. Someone else had phoned the police. She began sobbing again.

Pat had eaten in The Little Lunch House with Cameron that morning. Had Pauline been there with Kathy at the same time? Maybe the imaginary stalker wasn't so imaginary after all. She hadn't seen Sunny, but someone had followed her. She was sure of that now.

"Miss, get a full picture of the body," one official working forensics requested.

She did so. It was a scene similar to the others. The victim was lying on her side with her thumb in her mouth. A makeshift diaper had been fashioned from a towel, and this one had pins.

The body was naked and surrounded by pillows set up for protection from falling off the bed. She had been bathed, powdered, and lotioned, and her eyes were closed. She looked like a sleeping baby. The scene was fresh, so the overwhelming smell had not quite reached its foul peak in stench, and her hair was soaking wet.

Her hair was blonde. She was petite and weighed about 105 pounds, give or take. She was Caucasian and obviously another victim of the Baby Diaper Murders. Pat snapped the usual pictures. She was becoming an expert as of late. She knew exactly what was expected of her and snapped several that were not expected. She got a closeup of each pin fastening the diaper.

Oddly, the diapers were actually pinned to the girl's skin. The killer had no knowledge of actually pinning cloth diapers on a baby. One has to put their hand in the way, between the baby's skin and the pin, and do it gingerly.

The Baby Diaper Murderer had not done his job well if protecting the baby from harm was the plan. She snapped another closeup of the pins. She hoped that they had poked the gloves, giving a hint of what the perp's DNA might be. The murderer was bad at using them.

"Who did this to you, Pauline? What is the connection between you and the other girls? Is there a connection, or is this creep just picking you at random?" she spoke to the victim without expecting an answer.

She knew that she was missing something. They all were. What could it be? Cameron saw her and winked. She grinned slightly. If it had not been for the situation, she was sure that she would've thrived on the attention she was getting from him.

Instead, she heard his words in her head. He thought it was possible that Sunny was behind the murders. She shook off the thought and finished her work. When she had exhausted all the film, she gave the camera back to her new partner.

"How are you feeling?" she asked him.

"Better, thanks. I'll call you if this happens again. Do you have a cell?" he asked her.

"No, I'm sorry, I don't," she said.

"Here, take this beeper. If it beeps, it's me. Don't give the number to anyone else. I'll go back to the station and get another one for myself. I'll tell them I gave this one to my assistant," he said.

"What is your name again?" he asked.

"Patricia Farmer," she answered and gave him all the pertinent information required for her to be his assistant.

"I can't pay you very much," he explained.

"No problem. I just want to solve this thing," she answered. He nodded.

"Me too," he agreed.

They parted ways and let the forensic team finish so that the coroners could move the body to the morgue. Tony was in the back of the big black medical examiner's vehicle. He grinned at her and waved. She waved back, as her body betrayed her once again. On a whim, she walked toward him, which clearly surprised him in a pleasant way.

"Meet me by the water fountain when you're finished?" She asked. He nodded.

"Will two hours or so be okay?" he asked, trying to nail down a time.

"That's fine. Can you bring Mac? I want to go over what happened to her again," she mentioned.

"No problem. Is there new information?" he whispered. She nodded that there could be.

"Maybe," she spoke low and quick.

He nodded again, and she walked toward her dorm. She wanted Mac to go through the attack again. What was it that she had said? She'd heard her Sensei's voice in her head. Could he have been there, and she was too drugged to realize that he was the attacker? It was as possible as Sunny being the murderer. She just knew that everyone was missing something. She wondered what it was. What detail had been overlooked by every single person working the case.

She went to her dorm to write everything down in her journal. Perhaps she would read what she had been writing. Maybe she had unwittingly put a clue in there. Either way, she wanted to speak to Miss Tia Macalusa again and get the facts. Could her Sensei have been the man in that room with her?

Identity Theft: It's Murder!

CHAPTER FOURTEEN

P at sat on the edge of the wall surrounding the water fountain in the middle of the college campus anxiously awaiting the arrival of her friends. Should she tell Tony what Cameron suspected? She wanted to question Mac about the voices that might or might not have been in her head. Was she being foolish? Perhaps Cameron was right, and she was the one barking up the wrong tree.

Had Sunny really lied about being gay? Maybe she was bisexual and didn't understand the concept of it. Pat didn't claim to understand it, either, but she knew that many people lived their lives that way. Could Sunny not realize that she was bisexual, instead of just gay? Perhaps she was so desperate for affection that she had lied about everything else, too, to win her friendship.

Pat felt miserable. Had Sunny been the imaginary stalker as well? That was a little hard to fathom. She was big and clumsy, or was she? Perhaps that was just an act too. Pat sighed heavily, as she spotted Tony walking up the cobblestone walk toward her.

"Mac will be here in a few minutes." He explained why he was alone, even before she asked. She told Tony what Cameron had said about Sunny and what she had seen Sunny do at the Sound Rave. Then, she explained why she wanted Mac to go over the story. It was the voice she had supposedly "heard." Tony understood completely and agreed with Pat's assessment of Sunny's innocence.

Now, there was twice as much pressure to solve the crime. Not only had a friend as well as many others been killed, but also one friend was traumatized for life, and another was about to be falsely accused of the murders. It was all getting the better of her emotionally. She felt weak.

Tony admitted that, before now, it had all been a game to him. He had not been personally involved up until this point, but now Sunny was being affected as well as Mac. He'd grown very fond of Mac very quickly and didn't want to see her get hurt.

As he explained his position to Pat, she felt the same painful sensations she'd felt at the Sound Rave. She was jealous of Mac. She had to be. There was no other explanation for her bodily behavior. She squelched it, but the feelings were overwhelming with him this close to her.

He put his hand on hers and assured her that they would find the underlying cause of it together. Her entire body exploded at his touch. She couldn't control it. Her head began swimming, her toes tingled, and her breath was short. He'd said the word together, and it made her brain spin out of control and her heart pump for all it was worth. Her body was short circuiting and in complete malfunction mode. She was losing control of it all. What was happening to her? She jumped off the wall. She had no other recourse. He was stunned by the abrupt move, and it showed. He removed his hand from hers.

"Mac is here," she said hoarsely.

He looked at her through slanted eyes and tilted his head like a confused puppy. It melted Pat's insides, and she was glad his eyes averted to their oncoming friend. Mac looked tired and out of breath. The murders were taking their toll on her as well.

Pat composed herself while Tony and Mac exchanged greetings and small talk about their day. Pat joined in, as soon as she was able, and they walked over to a bench and sat down out of view and earshot of passersby. She tried to act as if nothing was wrong with her insides, as she pressed forward.

Pat asked Mac to repeat her story to the best of her ability. Mac obliged, once again mentioning Sensei's voice instructing her on how to disengage from her attacker just before she hammered him and fled the scene. That was the confusing part.

Pat listened, and Tony acknowledged her earlier statement. In theory, Mac was so drugged up that anyone could've been her attacker. She described him as "Frankenstein." Could it have indeed been her Sensei in that room? Being a karate instructor had to require amazing strength—so did being the perpetrator of the Baby Diaper Murders. The attacker had to have been strong enough to subdue the victim, to carry them dry into the bathtub, drown them, and then carry the soaking wet body out of the tub to the bed.

"Wait. The bed wasn't soaking wet, and neither were the diapers," Tony butted into the one-sided summation with his thought.

"That's a good point," Mac acknowledged, and Pat agreed.

"He must've let the water out of the tub and dried her off in there," Pat said thoughtfully.

"Yes, that's true. The tubs were all empty and scrubbed with bleach," Tony said, remembering the things he had heard on his end of the investigations.

"Still, it would require great strength," Pat said, not divulging her thoughts that it could actually be the Sensei and not the beast of Transylvanian legend. There was no need to upset Mac unnecessarily.

"You know what I think?" Tony interjected his thoughts again.

"What?" Mac and Pat asked at the same time.

"I think we need to learn a little bit of self-defense. Do you think your Sensei would teach us something in case...?" he asked Mac.

"In case what?" Pat asked incredulously. She had absolutely no desire to go near that karate school or any other one. She was kind and gentle, not that Mac was any different. It was just that fighting—mortal combat of any kind—was not in her. Mac had been doing karate since she was a little child. She had never known any other way. Pat had never even seen a karate school, never mind ventured into one voluntarily. She did not want to go.

"No, thanks," she added sternly.

"In case Pat gets grabbed, for one thing," Tony spoke over her, as if he was teaching a seminar, and she was talking out of turn.

"Mac only got free because she nailed the bastard in the face," Tony said bluntly to Pat in answer to her too quick response. It seemed logical to him. Not only could she check out her theory first hand, but she also might learn a little something in the process.

Pat knew she was defeated when Mac joined in to tell her it was a great idea. Mac had no idea of what the theory behind Tony's idea was; she just innocently believed that her good friend should learn karate in case she found herself face to face with danger. In her mind, it could definitely happen to Pat. Why not? It had happened to her, and she was a black belt. Pat finally conceded the point.

"You should come too," Pat said to Tony.

"Can't, got something else I need to do," Tony told her. "Mac will take good care of you," he added.

Pat felt that sinking feeling in her heart again. It was as if a big gooey, glue-like boulder rolled down from her throat to her stomach and filled her with a sickening, bloating ache. She watched Tony walk off in silent exasperation.

"Where do you suppose he disappears to?" Pat asked Mac without expecting a response.

"I don't know. The lair of the vampire maybe," Mac teased.

Pat nodded. That was her opinion too. One day she would follow him and see where it led her. She would probably take Mac too.

"Let's go over to the school now. I always help there after regular school. Come on," Mac said in her sixteen-year-old, karate enthusiast voice.

Pat trailed along, unsure and uncertain of what Tony had gotten her into. He had some nerve not joining her after all that. It ticked her off a little bit, but she said nothing. She wished silently that she had some way of contacting Cameron to let him know what was going on. She was frightened, but said nothing, as they walked to the parking lot and got into Pat's Buick. Wouldn't it be a hell of a thing to learn that her theory was correct and have no backup?

"Well, which way do we go from here?" Pat asked unenthusiastically.

Mac didn't seem to notice and gave her instructions, and they were off to the karate school. Pat felt anxious and apprehensive. She didn't want to go there, never mind under the pretense that she wanted to learn karate. What if the teacher threw her around the room and hurt her or something? Whether he was the perpetrator or not, that didn't seem like a farfetched idea of what must go on at a karate school. It was karate, wasn't it?

Mac babbled on incessantly about the wonderful people, the training being so much fun, and her life and growth at karate as Pat drove. Pat didn't speak, but did try to acknowledge her friend's excitement at bringing her into the world she had grown up in since she was very young.

Pat felt good that Mac felt comfortable enough to share that part with her, but it didn't alleviate her uncontrollable fear of the situation. There was too much at stake—her wellbeing, for instance

They pulled up in front of the karate school, which was hooked to an office supply store, and they shared the same parking lot. Pat brought the car into a spot directly facing the karate school, which was to the right side from that angle. She looked directly into the school through a huge picture window.

The building was whitewashed cement with giant red letters spelling "karate." They were the kind of letters that lit up at night. Pat wanted to turn and run, but Mac got out of the Buick and started up the walkway, which was the equivalent of a ramp for wheelchairs for handicapped people with a bright red banister. She took a deep breath and tried to smile, as she disembarked the Buick.

Mac smiled and beckoned her to move quicker. She was so excited; it was cute. Pat had forgotten for a while that Mac was still so young. She was so beautiful and so mature, but right now, she had an air of innocence. She had a child-like, little girl quality, as she smiled at Pat with her eyes sparkling in the clear blue color of a swimming pool. Pat smiled and continued up the walkway at her own pace. Mac urged her on.

It seemed as if time had stopped in that one minute so that Mac's true nature would be exposed to Pat—the little girl with deadly fists, legs that could level a Frankenstein monster, and a heart so sweet and still so innocent that it made Pat's own heart melt at the tenderness of it.

Mac held the glass door leading into the lobby of her second home open as Pat approached. Time caught up to itself,

123

as Pat took in the bright, homey lobby that Mac had come to love through the years. Mac was like a child with a new toy, and that made her even more beautiful. Pat grinned despite herself, thinking that so much loveliness in one person just wasn't fair to the normal people of the world like her.

The lobby had a hardwood floor with black chairs lining the wall against the side facing the parking lot. The classroom was behind a glass wall and could be clearly seen through the picture window Pat had looked through on arrival. Parents filled benches, and siblings played in a small room to her left. Directly in front of her was a small reception desk. An older woman with strawberry red hair tinted with gray sat behind it. She spoke on the phone with an enthusiastic voice, and she seemed happy doing her part to bring karate to the world. After she hung up, she noticed Mac and jumped up to hug her. They were clearly very close-knit.

"This is my second mother, Sempai," Mac said, introducing Pat to the woman. Pat smiled at the woman who was wearing a white top and black pants with a black belt wrapped around her waist.

"Sempai, was it?" Pat asked, repeating the woman's name.

"Yes, it's my karate name. It means older brother or sister, depending on who is wearing a black belt," Sempai explained briefly.

"Or everyone's mother, in your case." A male dressed in the exact same uniform, except that it was black, emerged from the glass-encased office located behind the reception desk. He put his arm around Sempai's shoulders and gave her a loving squeeze.

He was much taller than Sempai was, and Sempai was taller then Mac, not that she was tall, perhaps five foot one or two. The man in the black uniform had to be just shy of six foot, in Pat's opinion, and Sempai and Mac both looked up at him as if they adored him.

"This is Sensei," Mac said, introducing Pat. Pat glanced toward the mat. There was another man in the classroom. He was also in black. She could hear the laughter of the children he was teaching, and they seemed to be having a ball. She glanced back and forth between the two men.

"He's a Sensei too," Mac cleared up the question Pat had not asked.

Another woman dressed like Sempai came to the door separating the classroom from the lobby. She was of Hispanic descent with long, thick, black curly locks and eyes as black as coal. They were so dark that the pupils could barely be seen with the naked eye. She had olive skin and a pretty smile. She had a slight accent, as she called Sempai onto the mat to help Sensei and her with the children.

"Go with Betsy," Sensei said, giving her one gentler squeeze before shoeing her off in the direction of the mat.

Pat had originally seen Sempai as the parent and Sensei as the child. They had clearly reversed roles. It was a sweet scene. These people were far more than coworkers. They seemed like a genuinely loving family, although they were from every race and culture. It was as if none of the petty baloney out in the real world existed in this place. Pat liked the feeling. She felt at home, somehow, even though it was her first time on the premises.

Mac went into the locker room to change, while Pat sat in the office and talked to Sensei. His pool blue eyes were kind and warm, and the surrounding long black lashes gave him an air of innocence, although talking to him led her to believe that it was just an air and nothing more.

He was too thin to be mistaken for Frankenstein and clearly much better looking than the legendary manmade beast. Moreover, his head was clearly rounded at the top instead of flat, not to mention that no bolts could be seen on his neck. No visible stitch lines held his limbs in place, either. Apparently, he was put together correctly, and that was an understatement.

He gave her a card to fill out, and she did as he instructed, which seemed to be how each person in the building reacted to his commands. She instinctively knew that she was mistaken in her theory. There was no way that this good-looking, wonderfully gentle person would hurt anyone who had not tried to hurt him first.

"Sempai will take you through the building and show you where to put your shoes, and then we'll do a quick private lesson," Sensei said, taking the card back from her and making sure that it was filled out in its entirety.

Sempai came off the mat and right over to Sensei, as he motioned for her. He told her what to do, and she led Pat to the locker room, telling her about karate along the way. Another small classroom connected to the big one where she would be taking the private lesson with Sensei.

"You mean alone with him? Mac won't be there?" Pat asked, feeling cowardly, but not caring if she portrayed it or not.

"Yes, Mac will be on the big mat helping with the class," Sempai said with a gentle reassuring voice. "It'll be okay," she promised. "He's really a gentle man. He is powerful, but he doesn't use that unless there is no other way. It is a last resort. You'll see soon enough," she explained further.

The locker room was white tiles, mirrors, and a wall lined with sinks to wash your hands. There was a shower around the comer of the entrance and a small dressing room. The other side of the rectangle-shaped room was all light gray lockers with silver latches and numbers.

Pat picked one and put her things inside. She was being very quiet. She didn't know what to say to convey that she didn't want to do karate. She had only come to test her theory, and since that had been shot down, she just wanted to go home. She wished Tony were here so that she could choke him. This was his fault.

Another person in a karate uniform snuck up behind Sempai, as she spoke to Pat once they exited the locker room. He put his finger to his lips, telling Pat silently to be quiet. He got a bit closer and poked the older woman in the sides. He'd clearly startled her, and she screeched involuntarily. She turned to look him square in the face. His eyes were laughing, and so was his mouth. In Pat's mind, she thought that he would get along with Tony beautifully.

"This is Joshu. His main goal in life is to put me into an early grave," Sempai said and laughed, too, while swatting at him with an open hand.

''No, that's not the main one," he teased back, blocking the mock attack.

She gave him a wry look. He was of Hispanic decent as well, although his skin was darker than Betsy's was. His was like a milk chocolate brown. His hair was short, black, and curly. He had Betsy's eyes but he was taller than she was. There was no question that he was related to Betsy in some way. It turned out that she was his mother.

"His name is Joe Shoe?" Pat asked, separating the name as a first and then a last one as a purposeful act.

"It means assistant instructor. It is spelled differently than it sounds. J-o-s-h-u is the proper way to spell it. You can tell his rank by the black racing stripes down his shoulder," Sempai explained.

His white uniform jacket had black stripes the length of the arm, from shoulder to just below the elbow where the sleeve ended. The rest of his uniform matched Sempai's as well as that of his mother, Betsy. Another man dressed all in white with a blue belt wrapped around his waist walked by carrying a huge box full of different colored belts.

"Put those in the closet," Joshu instructed the guy.

"Osu, Joshu," the guy responded back in a military type of fashion. He had long brown hair that looked windblown. He wore glasses and had a decent build. Pat put him at about nineteen or so. He had a Southern drawl to his voice. Sempai introduced him as Phil. He didn't stop to chitchat other than a quick hello. Pat assumed that it was because the box was very heavy.

Sempai said that osu meant "yes," "hello," "good-bye," and "I understand" in karate language. Pat wondered how they would say a simple no. Although she felt certain they would say no extremely politely, she wondered if they said "not Osu" or something like that, but chose not to ask the question. She knew she'd figure it out in time all by herself, anyway.

Mac emerged from a door marked, "Girls." Pat assumed that it was the bathroom. She had on the same uniform as Sempai. She looked different, somehow. She carried herself with confidence. She knew who she was and was clearly proud to wear the uniform designating her rank. There was indeed a black belt wrapped around her waist too. Being told that she was a black belt and seeing her as one were two completely different things. It was astounding.

"Wow," Pat said, as she approached.

Pat decided that she was going to rework her vocabulary very soon. She had experienced a loss for words much too often lately.

"I see you've met the pain," Mac said, referring to Joshu. He put her in a mock headlock, and they struggled playfully for a few minutes while Pat and Sempai watched. Pat imagined that he was the annoying little brother of the group, the one who tormented everyone but was completely the object of everyone's undying love and affection. It was so cute and funny. This wasn't what she had pictured at all, not that it made her want to do karate any time soon, but she liked the atmosphere she was privy to because she and Mac were friends.

Sempai led her back to Sensei, while Mac went on the mat, and Joshu went into the tiny room where the siblings of students were playing with a clipboard full of papers to test students for belts. Sensei smiled and asked her if she was ready. She felt herself cower under his scrutiny. She felt intimidated and shy. She didn't want to be alone with him. He was much too good looking. He was not huge, but much larger than she was. What if he hurt her? What if everything she originally thought about karate was true? Would he be upset if she said that she wasn't ready? She cursed Tony under her breath, silently.

"I'm not sure," she stuttered.

"It's okay. We'll have fun. Just promise you won't hurt me," Sensei said.

She laughed at the silly comment that put her more at ease, and she followed him into the little room. She could see Mac clearly through the window, which put her even more at ease. Sensei sat on the floor. She did the same, twisting her legs into a pretzel. She remembered the words "criss-cross-apple-sauce" from when she was a child learning to sit that way in gym class, although she wasn't sure why; perhaps because she felt like a child at the moment.

"Mac says that there has been a rash of violent attacks at the college," Sensei began.

As they talked, she found herself opening up to him. He listened attentively, as she described the fear, yet didn't divulge that she was working on the case or the reason she agreed to come to karate in the first place. It felt good to release some pent-up fright she had been feeling for months now. He had heard the stories and seemed to care genuinely that she was afraid.

He assured her that he could teach her a few things in one hour that would help in a desperate situation. She found herself comforted and believing him. He wasn't rushing her. Instead, he let her go at her own pace. She got it all out in the open, and only then, did he offer to show her some karate. She agreed with less hesitation than she would have if they hadn't spoken first.

They started the lesson off by warming up their bodies. It was a good idea because exercise had not been at the top of Pat's list, ever. He said that she was doing well, and she told him that she'd been running a lot lately. She didn't tell him why. He showed her how to stand when in a confrontational situation.

He stood as a boxer might and then dropped one hand across his belly and put the other under his chin. He looked completely non-threatening. Then, he put his hands back up quickly. Mac stood like that all the time. She had never given it a second thought until that moment. She had been protecting herself in case, without alarming a would-be attacker in any way.

He showed her how to block first, then how to punch and kick. He told her that karate was defensive, not offensive. She liked that.

After that, he showed her how to get out of the two most common grabs an attacker might use. He then showed her how to palm heel at her request. He didn't ask why. She didn't offer.

She liked that he respected her privacy and didn't try to force her into giving him more information than she felt ready to give. When they were finished, they stretched out together. She'd had a wonderful experience. He had been patient and understanding, and he hadn't hurt her at all, except a few muscles that were sore already and would most likely be worse later.

She said good-bye to everyone after promising Sensei she'd be back for her first class. She had a karate uniform in her bag and a smile on her face. She had become part of Mac's second family that day. She felt good about that. She said good-bye to Mac, who had to stay and work and left to go back to the college.

It had been a wonderful endeavor, and she was now the newest member of the introductory course, which would last a month. Twice a week, she would don the uniform and train in the art of self-defense. It was so unlike her, but she was inwardly excited and thrilled to the core.

On her way out the door, another young girl walked in. She had on jeans and a baby blue sweater. Her hair was shining as if it had just been shampooed. The girl was slightly larger than Mac with a different eye color but clearly was Mac's sister. Pat smiled at her, as she continued on her way. She wondered vaguely if they called the young woman "Big Mac," and then laughed at her own joke.

Back inside the sanctity of her room, she wrote all of the new information in her journal. It was really coming in handy to write it all down. So much information was piling up. She wanted to find Tony and tell him that the Sensei theory had belly-flopped in one way and become a swan dive in another. She laughed at her own analogy, as she wrote it in her journal, saved it, and logged off for the night.

Tony found her, instead, although they never got to the conversation. She was sitting on her bed reading a book, and he just walked in. She was astounded. She couldn't believe that she'd left the door open. She was sure that she had locked it. She sat up quickly, and her nerves frayed on cue.

"Tony," she gushed in surprise. She grabbed her chest to stop her heart from getting out of it. The combination of primal instinct, where he was concerned, and instant fright like that made it pump harder than usual.

"Hi," he said with his wet red lips and sparkling eyes dancing in her direction. "I was wondering if you wanted to go out and grab something to eat with me," he asked. She calmed down in one way, and her body revved up in another.

"I really would, but I have so much reading to do," she answered with a frown that clearly said that she was bogged down.

"You are way too serious," he said, snatching the book from her hands.

"Very funny; give it back," she said, reaching for the book.

He had definitely lost her page. He smiled, and she believed for the moment that she had won the debate without a problem. He took a step toward her.

He brought the book back over to her and kept walking. He was walking right over her, as she sat on the edge of the bed. She tried to back up, but only her toes touched the floor and quickly, she found that she could not get out from under him. He continued forward with his knees on the bed. His legs were straddling her lap, and she was forced backward, but her feet were dangling off the bed from the knees down. He was sitting on her hips in seconds, and she dropped the book on the floor when he began tickling her. She was stuck!

"No," she squealed, cutting into giggles, trying unsuccessfully to fight him off.

Between spurts of involuntary laughter, protests, and pleas for mercy, she gave in and said that she would go anywhere, do anything, and see anyone to make him stop torturing her. He was clearly satisfied that he could get his way whenever he wanted and allowed her to continue working. She threw a pillow at the door playfully, as he exited the room. He ducked it with precise expertise, and she could hear him laughing all the way down the hall.

She hated herself for not minding the whole thing as much as she probably should have. She shook her head, locked the door, and returned to her work. Had he come just to tease her? Probably, she told herself and sighed. What was it about this guy? Why was her body betraying her at every turn? Her brain was now swaying as well. She knew that because the aftershock of her encounter was extremely pleasant, instead of her being upset like the "good girl" she was.

CHAPTER SIXTEEN

Two days had passed, and all was quiet when the beeper the photographer had given Pat went off in her pocket. She ran to the phone and dialed the number. The photographer answered. He was already en route to the crime scene. The Baby Diaper Murderer had struck again. Pat grabbed her purse and raced out the door toward the newest crime scene.

It wasn't long before she spotted a crowd forming around the dorm two buildings away from her own. Sunny's head stuck out above the rest, but Pat veered away from her to get to the scene quicker. Part of her noted that Sunny had indeed been at each scene quicker than, or right next to Pat. It unnerved her, but she pressed on.

Could there be something to Cameron's theory? Could her friend be that conniving and deceptive? If it were the case, she had certainly fooled Pat. The thought made her brain reel with confusion, hurt, and a little anger, but she quickly squelched it on arriving at the scene.

Cameron was there. He was not smiling. His jaw was so tight that a white line appeared where his jaw shut. He looked gaunt and pale. She knew that he wanted to solve the case and his frustration that the killer had not left so much as one clue to date. She also knew to her very core that his theory about Sunny had to be wrong. It was completely circumstantial, and she mentally kicked herself in the rear end for even entertaining the thought of such a thing. What kind of a friend was she turning out to be? No, Sunny deserved better than that. Cameron was wrong about her.

The photographer looked sicker this time than he had the last time, as he took deep gulps of water. Pat wondered what it was at each scene that seemed to be making him ill. Perhaps it was a clue. He had said that the Baby Diaper Murder scenes were the only ones where he felt sick. He shook his head and handed her the camera again. It was becoming a ritual with them, and she could see that he was thankful that she was there.

The scene looked just like all the others had. The young girl wrapped up in the blanket, accepting tea to calm down this time, was Cherie Klein. Cherie was a full-time student. She was studying environmental science, hoping to become a marine biologist just like the victim. Her roommate Carley was dead when she arrived back at the dorm from one of the field trips out to the ocean.

Carley was positioned the same as all the other victims had been. Pat took pictures and listened to the same questions that were getting officials nowhere fast. It was driving her crazy, and she could see what it was doing to Cameron. He looked very upset, and so did everyone else at the scene.

"What's that? Cameron asked, pointing waist level on the body. The officer handling the body looked closer, and he got excited. He held the body while someone else removed the evidence from it.

"Tom, look at this," one officer working the scene said, holding up a button in his latex gloved hand.

"Where did you get that?" Tom asked, as Cameron opened an evidence bag and let his fellow officer slide the button inside it.

"It was in the bed underneath the victim. Cameron spotted it," the officer who had found the button answered.

"The button was left there post mortem," one forensic official said, showing them the indentation of the button on the victim's body, which meant that the victim had already been dead when the button attached itself to her body. "And look at this; the button has lotion and powder on one side, yet not on the other;" the official continued, holding up the clear bag.

"The bastard dropped it at the end of his crime," Tom said with a grin. They finally had something to go on.

Pat took the photographs, as they spoke to each other. Everyone was thrilled that finally, the murderer might have screwed up and left a clue behind. Pat felt a sense of relief mixed with excitement.

The more they uncovered, the more it looked as if the murderer left the button. It matched nothing of the victim or her roommate, and Cherie didn't recognize it at all. At last, things were taking a positive turn, and it was about time—long overdue.

Pat spotted Tony helping with the body, and even he seemed impressed to hear that the murderer might have left a clue. It was only a button, but it was worth an elephant's weight in pure gold to the people trying to solve the case.

Once the investigation began to clear up, Pat left to go back to her dorm and relax. She'd felt so tired after they'd found the button. She wondered if that was a normal response to a positive turn in a case.

The crowd was dispersing, and she spotted Sunny still lingering about and headed toward her to say hello. She hadn't seen her in a few days. She waved and called Sunny's name. Sunny smiled and waved back. As she got closer to Sunny, she noticed that Sunny was wearing a silver gray shirt. Much to her dismay, the shirt was the same color as the button had been, and it was missing a button identical to the one found at the scene.

Tony caught up to her just then. In her shock, she had not heard him calling her name. His eyes got big, and the color drained from his face as he looked from the missing button to Pat.

"Hi, you guys," Sunny said cheerfully, unaware of what her friends were thinking.

"Hi, did you know that one of your buttons is gone?" Tony said in a hoarse dry voice, getting right to the point.

Pat couldn't believe that he just blurted the question out like that, but she looked at Sunny for an answer—not just any answer, but the one that would explain everything, like one where she dug a matching button from her pocket or something solid like that.

"It fell off when the crowd got thick, I think," Sunny explained. "It's probably on the ground somewhere," she added with a shrug of her shoulders. She glanced at the ground, but not for more than a second and dismissed the idea of looking any further for something as inconsequential as a lost button. Pat felt herself sinking into her own body. That was not quite the ironclad alibi she'd been hoping for.

Tony nodded as if he agreed with Sunny, but Pat knew better. That button was far from inconsequential. It was the only link to the perpetrator of the Baby Diaper Murders. Pat functioned as a robot and followed Tony away from the scene as if she were a little puppy on a leash following her master. She couldn't think; she couldn't feel; and she certainly felt lost. She felt like an idiot. She was a fool. She was beating herself to a pulp mentally.

Tony took her hand, bringing her back to reality, as her body reacted to his touch energetically. Normally, she tried to stop the reactions, but not this time. She needed to feel something, anything, to bring her out of the numbness that had threatened to overtake her just moments before.

It was too much to handle, though. The reaction to Tony was too fast and too strong, and all the sudden tears rolled down her cheeks as if a dam had burst through her eyes. Tony looked at her strangely. His eyes said that he had not wanted to be tangled in this web, yet he was tangled up in it. Pat did not know it, but he had fallen for her instantly. He chose not to go anywhere with it because he could see that she was interested in the police officer. He did not tell her that Mac had become the little sister he'd never had, and that although he adored her, he was in love with Pat. Mac was in love with someone at the karate school. He said none of this, but held her close to him instead and let her cry.

He stroked her hair and shushed her gently. Up until that point, he had also thought Sunny was innocent. Now, he didn't know what to think, as he held the weeping love of his life in his arms. He knew how close they were and how much Pat trusted her. He knew why she was so upset at the new turn of events.

Pat's body was beside itself reacting to the closeness she was experiencing with Tony. The silence was deafening, and the emotions made her cry harder. This couldn't be right. Something was desperately wrong. Everything was desperately wrong.

How could she be so chemically and physically attracted to Tony, her complete opposite, and yet want to be with Cameron? How could someone she loved and trusted as a friend have deceived her so thoroughly? Was Tony in love with Mac? Was Mac in love with Tony? How could she treat her friend this way? If Tony was Mac's, then she had no right to do this, to feel these things, yet she did. What kind of friend had she turned out to be? First Sunny, now Mac—was she this horrible of a person? Why had her whole life suddenly turned upside down? It was only a button, but it had pushed her into mind overload.

When all the parts of Pat finally calmed down, Tony pushed her hair aside and looked her in the eye. He held her face gently, and she put her hands on his.

"I thought she was innocent too," he spoke gently to his fragile love.

"Is it possible?" Pat asked, completely in the dark where Tony's feelings for her were concerned.

"There is only one way to find out," he said. That wild, crazy look that Pat had grown to know formed in his eyes. His lips became that wet red color. She knew he had something outrageous forming in his mind, as he usually did when he wore that look, but this time she was game. She was totally up for it if it could prove the innocence of her friend.

"How do we do it?" Pat dared to ask.

"By breaking into her dorm and having a look around before the police figure it out," he answered, raising his eyebrows.

"You're going to break in?" Pat asked, astonished.

"Not me... we, we are going to break in," he nodded his reply.

"Come on. We need to get some gloves and then stake out her place until she leaves," Tony said, taking her hand and not taking no for an answer, not that she was going to protest.

As crazy as she knew that the idea was, she also hoped that it might work and accomplish the goal of clearing their friend before Cameron told his theory to the superiors.

CHAPTER SEVENTEEN

Tony and Pat were dressed head to toe in black with latex gloves tucked into their sleeves. Pat knew that Cameron would kill her if he knew what she was doing, but she chose to look at the greater good. Moreover, she hoped secretly that he would never find out. When he scolded her, it reminded her of her father, and so far, that had been a complete turn-off because she was always in the position of defending her friend. The only thing was that when she was around him, she knew that she was safe.

Tony put his finger to his lips and motioned with his eyes. Sunny was on her way out. Pat could not seem to breathe, but remained quiet until Tony started out of the spot they were hiding in toward Sunny's door.

"Put your gloves on now," Tony instructed. She couldn't help wonder if he had done this before, but dared not ask.

"How're we going to get in?" Pat whispered, as Tony bent down toward the doorknob.

He picked the lock instantly by pushing a credit card into the doorjamb where the lock was.

"Just like that," he said and pulled her into Sunny's room with him.

They scanned the area. Pat wondered if that was how he'd gotten into her room the other night. She had been sure that she locked the door. It was routine to lock it at all times these days.

"Look everywhere," Tony said. "But don't mess anything. Put everything back where you find it. She can't know we were here, and neither can the police," Tony cautioned her.

Her heart was racing. She couldn't figure out whether it was the reaction to Tony or because she was a good person disguised as a burglar, breaking and entering someone's home without permission.

Tony was rummaging through the closet, checking pockets and shoes. She began opening drawers and checking notes, papers, and anything else she could without trashing the area. She checked the desk, the garbage can, and under the rug.

"Look at these," Tony said, holding up pictures of Sunny's family.

"She showed me those. Her mother sent them when she started gaining weight. Sunny and I noticed it right away. There was one that she didn't show me, though. She said that it was a terrible picture of her at the time," Pat said, crossing the tiny dorm room to look at the photos. The only ones that were there were the ones she had seen.

In the distance, sirens blazed, coming toward the college. Pat looked at Tony with fear and panic welling up within her. He put the photos back, and they exited the room. They quickly went back to Pat's dorm and locked the door behind them.

They removed the gloves, and Pat removed the black sweatshirt she had on. She had a pink tank top under it, and she folded the sweatshirt and put it away. Pat looked at her beeper several times. It had not gone off. If there were another murder, the photographer would've called her. If there wasn't another murder, why were the police pulling up in front of her building. Pat looked out the window. She saw Cameron and Tom along with several others.

"Do you think they know what we did?" Pat asked him in a frightened whisper.

Tony shook his head no. Within seconds, she knew that he was correct. Her beeper went off, and she called the photographer back.

There had not been another murder. Instead, the police felt that they had caught the murderer and were out to make an arrest. Pat knew that they were going to arrest Sunny, as the corridor carried the noise of the pending arrest in her direction. She went to the room that she had just left. The photographer was seconds behind her, and they went inside together. Moments later, Tony came in with no one suspecting a thing.

"Got something here," one officer said pulling the photographs from the pocket of Sunny's clothing in the closet.

"Got something here," another officer said strongly, as he pulled the silver gray blouse with the missing button from the hamper.

"Really got something here," Cameron said, pulling a crumpled up picture of a baby out of the trash pail. He flipped the picture over to show everyone in the room. The baby was in the exact same position as all the Baby Diaper Murder victims. The baby was wearing only a diaper. The name on the back was Sundance Joy, and it had her birth date written on it. Pat gasped aloud. How had she missed it? She was sure that she'd looked in the trash pail.

The horrible picture of herself that Sunny had hidden from her was the one of herself as a baby. The baby was lying in the exact same position the victims had been posed in. The other officers were not above being stunned.

They gathered all the evidence while Pat took pictures and Tony helped them bag it. Cameron was indeed the hero of the moment. His find had been the clincher. The picture was the evidence they had needed. They'd gotten the warrant based on the button. Apparently, Sunny had left a partial print on it. There was no question. When they found her, she would be arrested for the murder, but where was she?

Screams of anguish filled the corridor as the answer to her silent question. The room emptied quickly, as the officials raced toward it. Sure enough, another murder had taken place. Since Sunny did not know that a problem existed, Pat was sure that she would turn up in the crowd of people again. Even though all the evidence pointed to Sunny, Pat did not want to believe that she'd had any part of the murders.

Cameron stopped long enough to look her up and down on his way out. The look in his eyes made her feel on edge.

"You should get dressed if you're going to be part of these things. Do you think that I want all the guys to see you half dressed?" Cameron whispered and snapped the strap of her bra that was showing at the shoulder of her tank top. He was too close to her. She took a step back and wrapped her arms around herself. Was she undressed? Was she dressed in a manner that her mother would not approve of?

"I was in my room. I didn't expect to be here," she stammered for an explanation.

"I thought it was something like that, but next time, grab a shirt. You look like you're asking for it," Cameron warned. He kissed her on the forehead and continued on his way.

CHAPTER EIGHTEEN

P at positioned her camera to get a full tight shot of the body of a young woman whom had been murdered. The woman had short black hair; caramel-colored skin, blue eyes, and weighed one hundred pounds at the most. She was lying on her side on her own bed. She had her left thumb in her mouth as if she were a baby sucking it for comfort.

She was completely unclothed, except for a makeshift diaper fashioned from a towel and banana hairclips. Her eyes were closed as if she were sleeping peacefully. There were pillows on each side of her, positioned as if she were a tiny child that might roll off the bed and get hurt just like the crumpled up picture.

She was recently bathed, powdered, and had lotion on her as a loving mother might do to her infant. A chill shot down Pat's spine causing an involuntary shiver. It was the ninth scene of this type, and this time, one of her dearest friends was the accused. Could someone like Sunny have done this? Pat went over the facts in her mind, as she photographed the body.

The killing spree had come to be known as the Baby Diaper Murders. There was a serial killer loose, and no one could connect the victims in any way. They all had different jobs, took different classes at the school, or no classes at all. They were from completely different backgrounds. Their hair and eye colors were different. None of them had been raped. Some of them ate at The Little Lunch House, but did all of them?

The law officials did not believe that the murders were done completely at random, even though no pattern in the victims was emerging. Instead, they were sure that a serial killer was behind the crimes because the bodies were left in the same manner.

The question was the connection. They had not been able to figure out what they were missing. The answer eluded them, frustrated them, and remained unknown until they'd found evidence in Sunny's room.

The norm of serial killers is to kill the same type of person for a reason, wayward as it might be. This killer was not doing that. It was a spree of complete odyssey until the picture was uncovered. It was too convenient in Pat's mind. Someone was framing Sunny, but if that were true, why and who?

This current victim was eighteen, sweet and reserved, according to her friends questioned at the scene. She was a hairdresser who worked in the salon just down the street. She was taking courses at the college to better herself. Her name was Daniella Hernandez.

"Dani was the nicest person. Who would do this?" Pat heard one of the victim's friends say through an evolving sob, as Pat snapped another photograph.

"Your name was Dani?" she quietly asked the victim, not expecting a response while positioning the camera to get a closeup of the victim's face.

Pat's mind began churning. Events of the nine murders to date fell into place, as the thoughts spun haphazardly through the space-time continuum in her brain. She knew. She felt it. She had the answer. The connection that everyone failed to notice was right in front of her. The answer had been there all along. She lined up the facts, as she knew them, and the story formed from the first moment she'd found herself involved in it.

The connection was in the names of the victims, not the school or the diner. Each victim had a female name with a male nickname. Pat sighed. That theory even made Sunny look guiltier. Sunny couldn't have been a more male-oriented nickname.

Pat lined up more facts, as she photographed what she prayed would be the last murder scene of this type. Each girl was tiny. They weighed from 90 pounds to 110 or so. Strength was needed, but not as much as it would take to render a big woman helpless.

Mac had said that the person reminded her of the Frankenstein monster in her drugged state. Why had she used that particular analogy? She stuck to it, using it each time she described the memory. He'd worn a lot of clothes, she'd also said. Thick, soft clothes as Pat recalled.

Typically, serial killers were not female according to Pat's research. Although Sunny proclaimed herself a lesbian and dressed the part as well as acting it 99 percent of the time, she was still a female. She thought that went for her anatomical being as well, but there was no way to be sure. It had never come up.

She finished snapping the photographs and heard the walkie-talkie on Cameron's collar say that Sunny had been captured standing in the crowd outside the dorm. She was being read her Miranda rights and being brought downtown for questioning.

Cameron responded that he would follow shortly, to go ahead and book her. He and Tom would question her when they were finished at the crime scene. Pat thought that it sounded like something out of a bad movie.

Cameron received praise from the officer on the other end of the radio for a job well done. His fellow officers at the scene patted him on the back as well. He'd gotten the job done, and in all their minds, the murderer was in custody.

They were mentally closing the case of the Baby Diaper Murders without the benefit of a trial or a jury. Pat found herself wondering whatever happened to the old saying that Sunny was "innocent until proven guilty." She knew that they all thought that it had been proven, but in her mind, it had not.

Pat gave the camera back to the photographer, and he thanked her for all the help. She gave him back the beeper. He, too, believed that they had their man, or woman, as the case had turned out. Pat was beyond sad, beyond exhausted, and far beyond astonished. She sighed heavily and walked toward the door to leave the scene. Cameron stepped in front of her. He put his hands on her shoulders and kissed her on the forehead. She could see how happy he was and sensed his great relief at solving the case. She instinctively covered herself up with her arms the best she could.

"I have to take care of this nasty business, and then I'll call you," he said and scooped her into his arms.

"Sure," she said with no real enthusiasm. It felt like the touch a brother would have.

"Cameron, what if she didn't do it?" Pat asked softly. Cameron held her out far enough to look her directly in the eye.

"Honey, she is as guilty as sin. Haven't I proved that to you? You're just wrong about her. She took you in, that's all. You're not trained in this area. Now, go get dressed, and I'll call you when I'm through," he spoke to her condescendingly.

Even her father scolded her on an equal level. This was just too much to take. She said nothing and only half listened. She couldn't argue. It looked bad for Sunny. Pat wasn't even sure what to believe anymore.

She left feeling defeated and exhausted. Part of her felt dirty as well, for some odd reason. She covered her body again unconsciously.

"That smug bastard," Tony said into her ear, startling her out of her tired stupor.

"He's not smug; he's just right," she replied.

"Maybe," Tony said with a shrug.

"What do you mean?" Pat asked.

"It seems too cut and dry to me," Tony answered, looking troubled.

Pat didn't want to encourage him. She felt stupid about the whole thing. She had let her heart rule her head. The mistake described her life in one sentence. It was her biggest fault and often at the core of her problems.

"It is cut and dry," Pat disagreed. Cameron was right about everything, and they were wrong.

"Pat, snap out of it," Tony said, as he grabbed her and shook her.

"Give it up, Tony. The police have the right person," Pat said, removing his hands from her.

"What the hell is wrong with you? We can solve this together," he said with anger and incredulous disbelief building in his voice.

Pat turned on her heels and walked away from him without responding. She turned to look at him one last time before going around the corner, but he was gone. Tears found their way to her eyes once again. She felt completely upside down. She went into her room and tried to write in the journal, failing miserably. She pulled the sweatshirt out and put it back on. Even that didn't make her feel better.

Finally, she gave up and fell on her bed. She didn't like feeling duped, and she certainly hated feeling like a fool. Tony's words nearly ate her alive, as she tossed and turned into the sleepless night. Just before dawn, she decided to go and see Sunny at the jail. She would ask Sunny directly if she was innocent and then believe whatever answer she gave.

She would go to the karate school and pick up Mac if she would come. That way, perhaps Mac would remember something—some clue whether Sunny had done this terrible thing. After that, she would find Tony and apologize. That was the plan.

Pat did not go to classes the following day, nor did she answer the phone or respond to knocks on her door. She was too upset, too confused, and too unraveled. Instead, she lay in darkness with tears soaking her pillows and bedsheets. Was she this stupid, or was it that she was just this wrong? Without so much as a seconds worth of sleep, Pat waited until she knew that Mac would be going to the karate school to work and headed there too.

Mac was arriving just as Pat pulled the car into the lot. She beeped the horn to get Mac's attention. Mac scanned the area quickly after being startled by the noise. Pat knew that she, too, was on edge. She wondered if Mac was bouncing back and forth between guilty and not guilty, the way she had been since Sunny's arrest.

Mac loped along through the parking lot like a graceful gazelle toward Pat's car. Pat put her window down.

"Hi, what's up?" Mac asked, noting the dark sunglasses resting on Pat's very red nose.

"I'm going over to the jail. I was wondering if you felt like going too. I need to see if they truly have the guilty party here. She's my friend," Pat said with her voice cracking at the end of the sentence.

"I really do want to go. I need to see too. I want to know who attacked me. What if it wasn't her? He might still be out there," Mac said with total seriousness dripping from her tone.

"Get in," Pat said, opening the door.

Mac got in, and they were off toward the jail. Neither one of them could believe what they were doing. If someone would've told them a week ago that they'd be going to visit an inmate who might have committed the Baby Diaper Murders, instead of spitting nasty words at them, each would have laughed in the face of the person saying it.

They drove in silence for the forty-five minutes it took them to get to the jail—each woman tortured and tormented by thoughts of the inmate they were about to visit. Pat pulled into the walled lot of the jail and could not help notice the men with guns stationed high above them in towers on all four walls, not to mention the rolls of razor wire covering the top of the walls. The entrance was the only way in or out, and guards were stationed there too.

Once inside, Pat and Mac had to go through security, and finally, they were led into a rectangle-shaped room. They entered from the middle of one of the long sides of the rectangle. The rectangle was made of gray cement walls and had a long brick wall about three-and-a-half feet high cutting the room in half. On top of the brick was glass that went all the way up to the ceiling. The wall was cut into sections and had phones on each side of the glass so that visitors could speak to inmates, but they were not allowed to touch each other. On their side, little wooden stools were placed, one to a section. On the other side of the glass were people dressed in orange coveralls spread sporadically through the sections. Pat and Mac were escorted to the designated section the officer wanted them to use. They shared one stool while they waited patiently for the guards to bring Sunny out.

Sunny was escorted out, and Pat gasped at the sight. There was a chain around her waist and her hands were shackled to it. Another chain dropped from her waist to her feet, and her ankles were shackled to that. She could only take tiny steps while the unfeeling, insensitive correction officer pushed her along.

Pat and Mac exchanged a glance. Horror filled their eyes, as Sunny was pushed into her seat by the guard. The guard said something through clearly clenched teeth, but Pat and Mac could not hear what it was. Apparently, the glass was soundproof. Pat assumed that it must also be bulletproof. It would only make sense, given the quality of people forced to dwell in this God forsaken place.

Sunny's hands were freed so that she could talk, and she lit up when she saw Pat. They both picked up their end of the phone simultaneously.

"Hi." Sunny spoke first, and then huge crocodile tears fell down her cheeks.

"Are you okay?" Pat asked. Sunny sobbed gently and nodded that she was as okay as she could be under the circumstances. "What happened?" Pat asked.

"They found the button that I thought I lost in that huge crowd that had gathered at the last murder, and then they found a bunch of stuff in my room, including a picture of me that they say I crumpled up and threw away, only I didn't do it," Sunny answered truthfully.

"There was another murdered victim found after the one with the button, wasn't there?" Mac whispered. Pat nodded.

"Did you do this?" Pat asked her directly.

"No. I couldn't. I would never," Sunny stuttered and cried harder. It was a pathetic, sad, tormenting thing to watch, as Sunny fought to control her emotions but failed miserably.

"Real killer material," Mac whispered again. Pat took a deep breath. Her friend had not committed the crime. It was such a relief. Now, the truth had to be uncovered.

"Sunny, is there anything you know that could help us find the real killer?" Pat asked, knowing that there was probably nothing but that it was worth a shot.

Sunny shook her head no, sobbing again into her end of the phone. Her eyes told a thousand tales of fear and sadness. Pat knew without a doubt that Sunny just had to be innocent, and if that were the case, then the real killer was still on the loose. She intended to talk to Cameron about it as soon as possible, that is, right after she apologized to Tony. She had reacted like a jerk, and she knew it.

Pat put her hand up to the glass, and Sunny did the same.

"I won't rest until I find out who put you here," Pat vowed quietly but sternly.

"Thank you," Sunny replied, wiping her eyes on her sleeve.

"I need to talk to her for a second," Mac whispered and motioned for Pat to hand her the phone. Pat complied with her request but was confused by it.

"Hi, Sunny, my name is Tia. We met once at the club," Mac said, using her proper name. Sunny nodded.

"I was just wondering how your nose was feeling. I heard that you got hurt," she said, scrutinizing Sunny's eyes for any sign that would show she knew what was being talked about.

"My nose got hurt? No, it's fine. They hurt my arm, not my nose," she said, pulling up her sleeve enough to show Mac a huge black and purple elbow. Mac gasped.

"Oh, I must've misunderstood. Is your arm okay?" she lied and then asked, astonished by the bruising and swelling obviously not seen by a medical professional. Sunny nodded that she'd live, and Mac nodded back while trying to smile at her for moral support.

"It wasn't her. She had no reaction to my hitting the killer's nose with my palm heel," Mac assured Pat who had already come to the same conclusion.

Pat nodded. She spoke to Sunny gently, encouraging her and telling her to keep her chin up. Sunny promised that she would, just as the phones went dead. They hung up, and Pat blew her a kiss as the guards came and shackled her legs and hands to take her back to her cell. Pat and Mac went back out to the parking lot in silence. Both turned over thoughts in their head about who the real killer might be.

A woman walked toward them pushing a stroller through the parking lot.

"Nice place for a baby," Mac said—Pat's exact thought at the moment.

As the woman drew closer, Pat realized that it was Tiffany-Crystal, Sunny's mother. She had changed a bit but was recovering her figure nicely.

"Is that you Mrs. Chyna?" Pat asked, hoping that she was not mistaken.

"Yes," the woman half asked in response.

"I'm Patricia Farmer. I drove Sunny to college. Do you remember me?" Pat asked.

"Oh, yes, dear, of course, I do," Tiffany-Crystal sang.

"Is this the new baby?" Pat asked, looking into the stroller.

"Yes, this is my little Ralphie," Tiffany-Crystal sang out proudly.

Pat could not help wonder if she would've been quite so sugary if little Ralphie had been a little Ralfette.

Tiffany-Crystal picked Ralphie up out of the stroller so that the girls could get a better look. He was indeed beautiful. He looked so much like his mother. He was tiny with sweet features and silky blond strands of hair.

He made a small cooing sound, and both girls joined Tiffany-Crystal in momentary awe of the little bundle from heaven. Pat wondered, without saying, how Ralph Senior would react if his long-awaited son was as much like Tiffany-Crystal as Sunny was like him. It would be interesting to see.

"Where's Big Ralph? Is he parking the car or something?" Pat asked, scanning the parking lot.

"No, he's not here. The bowling league has their annual tournament coming up, and the men need to practice," she answered, as if she didn't have a care in the world, instead of a daughter who was in prison facing murder charges.

"Mrs. Chyna, Sunny didn't do this," Pat said, almost defending her friend against her vile father's choice to go bowling, instead of supporting his only daughter in her time of need.

"Oh, I know that, dear," Tiffany-Crystal said and waved her hand as if she were a queen.

"If she was that kind of a person, I'd have known long before now. We're from a small town, you know. It would've arrived at our house five minutes before she did, if you know what I mean," she said, placing Ralphie back in the stroller and fastening the belt that kept him safe.

"When I went to the doctor to find out if I was pregnant, the nurse knew why I was there before I mentioned a word. The whole town knew," she continued with a slight giggle tucked into her words.

"Right now, our name is mud in the town, though. Sunny's indiscretion or involvement or whatever you want to call it has done none of us any good," she scolded, seeming to come to a more serious place in her twit-like brain. Pat thought that it was about time she'd come to that.

"She's innocent, though; you know that, right? The indiscretion wasn't hers," Mac interjected with disdain forming in her tone. She clearly found Tiffany-Crystal's attitude below reproach. So did Pat. Was the woman on drugs or something? What kind of a mother was she? Pat wanted to scream at her to show a little faith in and support her only daughter.

"I'm sure she is, dear. I talked Ralph into giving me the bail money. I want to take her home where we can hide her for a while," Tiffany-Crystal said, adding a "Tata, ladies" to her ending sentence, and she went on her way.

"Poor Sunny," Mac said, exasperated and with her jaw hanging open like a gaping black hole. Pat nodded, and they went on their way. Pat felt frustrated and wondered where to begin to find the evidence that would prove Sunny's innocence.

"Do you want to go home or to the karate school?" Pat asked Mac, as they got closer to home."

"Take me to the school. I'm going to have some explaining to do about skipping out on work with no notice," she answered apprehensively.

"They won't fire you, will they? Blame me," Pat offered.

"They can't fire a volunteer. It would be weird," Mac said with a grin.

Pat smiled back. At least the life of one of her friends was still intact. She let Mac out at the school and waited until she got inside to leave. She locked her doors and headed back to the college. She hoped to see Tony so that she could apologize for being such an emotional stooge. She was sure that he'd forgive her, but she wanted to say the words anyway.

CHAPTER NINETEEN

Tony sat in one of the booths at The Little Lunch House waiting for Mac. Meeting her after work had become almost a ritual.

Mac came in windblown, tired, and smiling. She had been waiting to talk to him all day. They ordered burgers and malted milks, which had become a favorite evening meal for them while they talked.

Seconds after the order was delivered to their table, Tiffany-Crystal came in and sat at the counter with Sunny, pulling the stroller close to her so that she could keep a close eye on her sleeping baby.

"That's Sunny's mother. Sunny got out on bail," Mac whispered to Tony, pointing discreetly at Tiffany-Crystal. "It must've been an astronomical amount of money considering the charges," she added. Tony turned around slowly and took a quick peek.

"Wow," he said with his eyebrows raised and a surprised look on his face. He looked at Mac and wondered if she were joking. There was no way that was Sunny's birth mother.

Mac crossed her heart and put one hand in the air showing three fingers as if she were a scout swearing in an initiation ceremony, while nodding her head purposefully exaggerating the movement to make her point.

"Mix-up at the hospital maybe?" Tony whispered back with a grin. Mac slapped his hand.

A police officer came in and sat a few seats away from the mother and daughter. Sunny's face showed complete mortification, as Tiffany-Crystal struck up a conversation with the officer. She just didn't like cops at that time. It was understandable. How could her mother be so insensitive to that?

Tiffany-Crystal and the officer shared niceness and kindness, and then Cameron's name came up. Sunny couldn't hide, but there was no doubt that she wanted to.

Tiffany-Crystal told a story of Cameron as a little enterprising young man who had stolen the bicycle of a boy in town, and then talked the boy into paying him to find the bike. Apparently, it had all been going pretty well until his father found the missing bike in their basement. Cameron had a sore bottom for a week. Tiffany-Crystal and the officer were laughing.

"The boy just wanted to be a hero. Who could blame him with parents like that," she continued, joking with the mesmerized officer.

"What do you mean?" the officer asked, making mental notes to tease his fellow officer at the first opportunity.

"Well, they were both war heroes, C.J. and Antoinette Scott; you might be too young to remember," Tiffany-Crystal announced.

"Well, you couldn't be more than twenty years old yourself," the officer complimented her.

The server then showed her unwavering admiration by telling them that Cameron fed the homeless on a continuous basis. He gave them money too. He'd taken a special interest in one of the worst of the bunch, she confided in a whisper but making sure that she was loud enough for everyone around them to hear. That person was a lunatic, according to her expert rendition of the situation. "Probably schizophrenic," the server finished her story with a wide-eyed nod. She then swooned dutifully and said that he was so wholesome that he reminded her of freshly baked bread and more gorgeous than anyone she had ever seen. The rest of the servers agreed as well. He was already a hero in this town, as far as any of them were concerned. Sunny looked as if she wanted to be sick.

Tiffany-Crystal agreed through a lighthearted chuckle and said that she thought that his uniform was part of the allure now, although he'd always done well without it. He'd been one for the ladies in the small town that they called home, that was for sure. The servers swooned on cue and huddled for more gossip on their current, real-life hero.

Tony put his finger to his mouth as if he were going to try to commit suicide by gagging himself. The last thing he wanted to hear was what a wonderful family Cameron had come from. The guy had it all. He was good looking. He was a police officer, known and well respected now that he had been an intricate part of solving the rash of murders on the college campus. His new hero status would most likely open political doors for him if he chose to go that way, but what was worse than all that was the fact that he had Pat's attention and apparent devotion. It just didn't seem fair that on top of all that, his parents were decorated war heroes. It sickened Tony, and he didn't want to hear another word of it.

"I need to get out of here before I toss my cookies," Tony whispered. Mac nodded and understood, although Tony had not spoken the words aloud. She knew Tony well these days, and it was no secret to her how he felt about Patricia Farmer. There was no question in her mind that Tony was in love with Pat. She wished in silence that she could help, but she instinctively knew that it was better not to get involved in matters of the heart when her own heart was not involved in the love part.

They listened for another few seconds about the Scott family being important and well known, and then Tony dropped the money on the table to pay for the meal. The look on his face matched what Mac was feeling. Tony and Mac finally got as sick of the conversation as Sunny looked and ducked out of the diner.

Tony walked her home and then disappeared into the shadows for the night, as Mac watched him leave. She kidded herself with the possibility that he really was a vampire or some other kind of creature of the night that supposedly existed, except that he walked in daylight. She wondered if he saw a reflection when he looked in the mirror.

She adored him, as one would love a favorite uncle or a big brother, but she had often wondered since she met him where he called home. She decided that one day, she might follow him just to find out the answer to that question. Perhaps she'd get Pat to go with her. She figured that the thought had crossed her mind at some point as well.

Pat wrote in her journal until her fingers hurt from typing. She had a lot of catch-up entry to make. She had let her confusion and emotions overwhelm her to the point where she could barely function for a while, but that was over with. Her main goal now was to find the real Baby Diaper Murderer and prove Sunny's innocence. She fully intended on finding Cameron and asking him, begging him if need be, to help her.

She logged off and found her way to her pillow. On this night, she slept easily and soundly. Tomorrow was another day. It would be an important day—the day when she would find the evidence to clear her friend and put the real killer behind bars where he belonged. She felt better.

P at went to the police station directly following classes the next day. She just had to talk to Cameron and enlist his help in her endeavor to find the real killer behind the Baby Diaper Murders. She was led to his desk in much the same manner as she had been the last time.

The pile of mess that had occupied the top of the desk hadn't changed much, but there were three bouquets of flowers with congratulations balloons and festive-looking decorations, as well as numerous hero jokes extrapolated from the Internet. Pat looked at all of it without moving from her chair or touching it.

She guessed that finding that final clue had brought the rookie officer to real hero status among his fellow employees, even more so than she had realized. She was happy for Cameron, but she wondered how willing he would be to listen to her proclaim her friend's innocence and then how cooperative he would be when she tried to enlist his help.

Pat let her mind wander a bit and thought about the relationship that they had begun building the day she'd seen him get sick in the hallway after seeing the first murder victim. She remembered thinking that he was so sensitive and finding that extremely attractive. She had been so excited when he'd finally asked her out for a date. It was almost disappointing that the relationship had not blossomed any further since then. He seemed so perfect for her. He was handsome, smart, kind, and a true gentleman as far as she was concerned. She couldn't help

163

wonder why the stars and rockets she'd heard so much about had never appeared. Heaven knows that she wanted them to.

She figured that it might be because they had both felt so pressured to solve the Baby Diaper Murders. Though their reasons for wanting the culprit caught were very different, the goal had been the same and required much energy to accomplish. Perhaps she hadn't really given the relationship enough of her attention. She intended to remedy that soon—hopefully, right after the real killer was caught.

"What a nice surprise," Cameron said, approaching the desk. His eyes lit up, and he was clearly happy to see her sitting there.

"The hero always gets the girl, doesn't he?" one of his fellow officers teased from across the room, sailing a paper airplane in his direction. Cameron smiled and laughed, as the airplane hit him on the abdomen. He opened it. It was yet another hero joke off the Internet.

"Don't pay attention to them. What brings you here?" he asked, gently urging her on. He could see that she clearly felt out of place. He thought that it was adorable. She was blushing slightly, crossing her legs while tugging on her shirt a bit with one hand, and clutching her purse in the other.

He'd wanted her from the moment that he had met eyes with her in the hallway of the dorm. He could tell that she'd liked him too. He could see them becoming an unstoppable team, with him solving the crime and her photographing each step. The thought completely engulfed him for a second, and his heart did a happy little spasm at the thought of it. She had promised him unwavering worship if he'd solved the case. There was no question that he had definitely accomplished that goal.

"Truthfully, Cameron, I wanted to talk to you about the Baby Diaper Murder case," Pat began. He had no problem with that. It had become his favorite subject. He put his elbows on the desk, rested his chin on his hands, and gave the impression of undivided attention toward her.

"Why, do you want his autograph?" another officer said, and the rest laughed along, taunting Cameron in a male bonding fashion.

Pat was regretting having come, but since she was there, she forged ahead. She just had to tell him that it wasn't over. He had to know that they had the wrong killer and her certainty of that. She hardly knew where to begin.

"I was wondering if we haven't made a big mistake," she said half in question form.

He looked dually shocked, and a red hue formed on his cheeks. She hadn't meant to embarrass him, but clearly, she had, anyway. He regained his status right away at her expense, however. You could've heard a pin drop at the station. There was complete silence, except a few snickers in the background.

"What have we made a big mistake about?" Cameron asked her with a voice that an adult would use to indulge a child.

Pat was getting frustrated but continued. Perhaps once she got it all out, he would see her point. She explained about going to the jail, but did not mention bringing Mac. She was only sixteen, and she could clearly see that he was not happy that she had gone there herself. She then tried to reason with him about the clues being rather conveniently placed.

"You're just upset, Patricia," Cameron said, taking a deep breath and rolling his eyes.

The officers agreed with him and laughed openly at her expense as well. "I know you thought that she was your friend, but sweetheart, she's as guilty as they come. You go on home now, and I'll call you later, and we'll have a nice talk about it," he reassured her in the same condescending manner.

She knew that she was getting nowhere fast, so she nodded her head. He kissed her forehead, adding insult to injury in front of his friends and dismissed her accordingly. By the time she started her car, she was seething with anger. How could he have treated her like that? She felt like such a fool, and why hadn't she been stronger and fought him on it? Why hadn't she taken a stand for her friend's innocence? Why did he call her honey and sweetie? What was that all about? He'd treated her like a spoiled child that needed a band-aid for a nonexistent injury.

Her mother would've been proud, she thought angrily. She had acted like a perfect lady. It was too bad that that fact did not spark any pride in her. She was angry with herself for being such a wimp.

She decided to go over to the karate school and have a workout. She was mad as hell, and she needed an outlet. She was glad that she had not yet removed the uniform from her car.

Mac was already inside talking to Sempai, who was checking in students at the reception desk. The lobby was full, and the topic of discussion was the same one that had Pat's head spinning. It was about the Baby Diaper Murder case. Sunny's picture was on the front page of *The Observationist News.* Cameron's was on page three.

Pat checked in, but did not join the conversation going on. She'd had all that she could take of that subject at the moment. Listening to the women in the lobby of the karate school swoon over Cameron would just be beyond what she could handle mentally. She went into the locker room to change into her karate uniform, which she had recently learned was called a Gi.

"He's the son of war heroes," Mac said, as the crowd looked at Cameron's picture.

"No, he's not," Sempai informed the crowd.

"What do you mean?" one woman in the lobby asked.

"I did a report on them when I was a kid. I was in the second semester of college, I think," Sempai said, remembering the story as it had taken place about twenty-six years earlier.

She told them that the original story about Carroll John III also known as C.J. and Antoinette, alias Toni, Scott had been the one depicting them as war heroes. Those weren't even their real names. It had turned out sadly that the children Antoinette had protected were carrying microchips sewn into their skin, giving the enemy American military secrets. The man C.J. had shot was the American agent that had found the trail leading to them. Their big mistake was leaving him for dead. He not only didn't die from the shot in the head, but he lived to warn our government. He died after that. He was the real hero. His name was never divulged.

No one had noticed the heroes being the bad guys because the good story was written with their new names, and the real one was written months later with their actual names. Sempai had put the stories together, along with the photographs. and had received an 'A' on the report.

The crowd in the lobby listened in awe. Sempai said that she still had the report, complete with the works cited page that told exactly where she had gotten the information if anyone wanted to see it. She had found it accidentally herself back then while doing research. Several people gave her their e-mail addresses, and the rest just took her word for it. She wasn't one for fabricating stories about people. They knew that her background saw to it that the real stories in her life were compelling enough when she told them.

Mac was shocked. She knew that Pat was seeing him, and she was sure she cared deeply for him. She wondered if Cameron knew the truth about his parents. She wondered if she should tell Pat. She decided to ask Tony's opinion before she did. He was a little older and knew Pat better than she did; and in her opinion, he loved her. That meant that he wouldn't hurt her purposefully. He would know whether to say anything.

Pat emerged from the locker room and joined the others filing in on the mat in the classroom. She couldn't wait to begin. Her neck was tight, her shoulders were sore, and she needed to empty her overreactive mind for a while and concentrate on learning something new.

As if Sensei had heard her, he explained to the room full of beginner students that the hour in class was a mini-vacation from the world. They were to leave everything outside the door whenever they came, and when finished, they would go back with energy, zest, and perhaps even a different, fresh perspective on things happening in their respective lives. She heard Sensei loud and clear. She was ready.

After class, Pat found herself drenched with sweat and feeling much better. It was almost as if she were on a natural high. Sempai explained that exercise released endorphins into the body. Endorphins were healthy secretions in the brain, with the side effect of making a person feel happy. Pat knew that, or at least she'd heard it before somewhere, but she'd never experienced it before. She had never worked out like that before, either. She was glad that she had joined. Karate was nothing like anything she had ever imagined.

She said a hearty good-bye to all her new friends and then to Mac and headed for the college. She wanted to read all the entries in her journal and see if she'd written something that had gone unnoticed the last time she tried. She felt more aware and more focused than she had last time, too, and she hoped that would give her a new perspective on the things she had written. That seemed to be a side effect of the endorphins as well, and Pat was thankful for it.

She was walking from her car to the dorm when she saw Tony sitting on the wall of the water fountain.

"Tony," she called out in a relieved voice. She'd wanted to tell him that she was sorry for being such an idiot the other day. Her stomach did an involuntary jump in quite a pleasant manner, and her heartbeat sped up just at the mention of his name.

She wished that she could control her reactions, but she didn't really mind them anymore. She looked forward to them sometimes, and she had missed them since they had disagreed about Sunny.

"Hey, what's up?" he asked, as if nothing had occurred between them. "I was looking for you," he added. Pat stopped short, and her body went nuts. Tony had been looking for her? What on earth for?

"Well, you've found me," she answered awestruck. She sat on the wall of the water fountain. He stood in front of her with his hands jammed into his pockets.

"Look, I didn't want to get this involved with you," he began. Pat's heart sank. It almost sounded as if they were breaking up, except they weren't going together. "I thought we had a lot in common, and it was fun to do those crazy things together," he continued. Where was he going with this? Pat's throat filled with a thick layer of that glue-like goop, and try as she might, she could not swallow it. Should she apologize quickly and stop the emotional freight train from tearing her heart out? "I had no intention of… of," he stammered for the last half of the sentence.

"You had no intention of what?" Pat asked confused.

"1 don't know—of getting in so deep," he answered. His eyes looked at her as if he were pleading with her to get it. Unfortunately, "it" escaped her. She had no idea what he was talking about. "I can't walk away, get it?" he asked with a bit of anger or resentment rising up in his voice.

"No one's asking you to walk away," she assured him, still not quite understanding where he was coming from. "I'm so sorry for being such an idiot the other day. I was just confused or something," she began to explain.

He stepped close to her and put his arms around her hips. The moonlight made his hair shine and his eyes sparkle. Her entire nervous system, not to mention all her other systems went into some kind of electric short-circuit mode. He brought his lips to hers and kissed her.

His lips were sweet, moist, and warm. Fireworks went off in her brain for all they were worth. Stars and rockets flew too. So, this was what all the hubbub was about. She now understood what the big deal was, or at least her body did. He leaned in closer, and she found herself responding in harmony to his kiss. Her hands slid around his neck and drew her into the most magical mode she had ever known in her lifetime.

They were getting heavy into the moment when Tony leaned in too far, and they both flipped into the fountain. The water was very cold, and the shock brought them both back into reality. They came up laughing. Pat splashed water at him, and then he splashed water back at her. They got into a splashing match when he grabbed her around the waist, pulled her close to him, and they kissed again. Pat found that she was grateful for the coolness of the water. It helped her maintain some control over her body, even though she was shivering. It was amazing, and she believed that Tony was the one she had waited her entire lifetime to meet.

She knew that nothing even close to that feeling had ever
occurred when she was with Cameron. He was a great guy,
but he was only that. She knew to her core that Tony was the
one who held her heart, and now, he was holding their whole
bodies very close as well. Her body was so close to his, it was as
if they were one. She'd never been that close to any male before.
She knew that she hadn't ever felt this way before, either. She
wanted to do wild and crazy things with him. It was an odd
sensation she did not divulge with words. Still, somehow she
thought that he knew what he was doing to her. She had the
strangest urge to wrap one of her legs around him, though
she did not act on the notion. The sensations were new and
exciting and coming on strong.

He pushed her wet locks aside and kissed her a third time
before a security vehicle came by and told them to get out of
the fountain before he wrote them up. They complied, and he
drove off, shaking his head, although the grin on his face led
them to believe that he wasn't that upset.

"Can I walk you home?" Tony asked with his hair dripping
and a grin on his face.

"Tony, I've never... I mean... I'm not that kind of a girl,"
she said, wriggling from his grasp. He nodded. He'd figured
that out long before now.

"I'm not asking to bed you down right here. I just want to
walk you home. I'm not ready to end this night just yet," he
said, taking her hand in his.

They walked together toward her dorm, leaving drops of
water on the cobblestone in their wake. Pat had never been
happier than she was right then. The funny thing was that her
happiness paled in comparison to Tony's; at least he thought so.

When they got to the door of the building, he swept
her into his arms and kissed her again. Her body melted and
conformed to his. She didn't want it to end. Her head was

spinning. The rockets and stars she had always dreamed of appeared in the mystical aura in her mind. She pulled him closer to her and gave back what he was giving. When they finally parted, he stared at her for the longest minute of her life.

"If I don't leave you now, I won't leave," he said in a breathless whisper. He didn't wait for a response. He walked away and disappeared into the shadows without looking back. She had to fight to control her breath. It was as if she'd run a marathon.

She watched the shadow in the area where he disappeared for a few minutes. Part of her hoped that he would reappear. If he did, she told herself that she was going to bring him up to her room. She was a grown up after all, and she definitely wanted him in a grown-up way.

She almost felt disappointed that he didn't come back, and she finally went inside. She wondered what it would be like if he really touched her. She wanted him to touch her and to kiss her, hold her and to love her. She sucked in a huge burst of air, finding herself in the position of craving something she'd never had before. She felt exuberant and wonderful. She hugged herself while she was still wet before she peeled her clothes off and hung them in the bathroom.

The phone rang, as she logged on her computer, and she answered it, hoping that it was Tony. It was Cameron. Her mood crashed, but she tried not to let him hear her disappointment.

"I was worried about you. I called a bunch of times," he said in an accusing tone.

"I went over to the karate school to see Tia," she said, being very careful not to use her nickname, although she wasn't sure why she felt compelled to do that.

"I don't think I like the idea of your wrestling around with a lot of sweaty men," he said disapprovingly. She pretended not to notice the tone and did not acknowledge the statement. How had their relationship evolved to this level in his mind? The whole middle was missing. The good part had never occurred. He just ordered her around at will. He told her what was appropriate to wear, who her friends were allowed to be, what kind of exercise she was not allowed to do—was he kidding? She continued explaining, though she wasn't sure why she was doing that, either.

"And then I met Tony outside by the fountain, and we talked for awhile," she added, telling a half-truth, as the realization of being scolded like a child again hit her. She knew that she was playing with fire here, but she also felt that she shouldn't need to feel that way. She wanted to tell him the truth about her evening with Tony, but she felt that she should wait until she could see him in person. For some strange reason, she felt as if she were being put on the spot or being interrogated in a way. The more they spoke, the more she knew he was not "the one" for her.

"Is he the one filling your head with all that crap about Sunny being innocent?" Cameron asked in a cool voice. Pat felt immediately defensive. What on earth was happening here? Was she talking to her father or a guy she had dated a few times? No one "filled her head" with anything.

"No, that was all me. I think we might be making a mistake, Cameron," she said in a gentle tone, not that he heard her or would even entertain the thought if he had. In her mind, she added the sentence, "in every aspect of the word." She was thinking about their dating relationship as well, not just of Sunny's innocence.

"Baby, she's guilty. I know it's hard, but try not to think about it. How about we meet at The Little Lunch House tomorrow—say 6 o'clock?" he offered, as if he were giving a child a piece of candy to appease her at the end of a temper tantrum.

She cringed inside, as he spoke. She wished that he'd stop with the ridiculous pet names. She couldn't stand the condescending tone, putting the little woman's silliness to rest. They'd only dated several times, for heaven's sake. He was acting as if they had been married for ten years.

She knew that no matter how hard she tried, she would never be able to make herself react to Cameron the way that she naturally reacted to Tony, but she agreed to meet him at the diner. In her mind, she was going to let him down easy, offer her friendship, and explain that it just wasn't right between them; at least it wasn't right for her.

She hung up with him and wrote in her journal about the evening's events. She dwelled on her feelings about Tony as if she were trying to sort them out for herself. She confided to the pages of her journal her innermost desires where Tony was concerned, and she realized full on that she was truly and totally in love with him. She didn't know much more about him other than that, but he had won her over, lock, stock, and barrel. Her heart, her mind, her body, and her soul belonged to him, and she was counting the seconds until she could kiss him again. He was the first man she'd ever thought about giving her most precious gift to, and the feeling astounded her. Since the proper words didn't exist to describe her feelings, she just wrote them out as plainly as she could.

Mac called her shortly after she logged off to say that she wanted to help Pat in any way she could to prove Sunny's innocence. She added that Tony felt the same. Pat grinned, remembering her evening and thinking about her secret desires.

"Okay, find him. I have to see Cameron at the diner at six, and I'll meet you at the Sound Rave tomorrow night at seven.

I'm going to try to recruit Cameron's help. We'll get right to work," Pat agreed.

She figured that an hour would be enough time to tell Cameron her true feelings and then make a graceful exit. He wanted no part of helping Sunny, but she would ask him one more time, anyway, and offer to let him join Tony, Mac, and her in their quest to find the truth. Although she was sure that he would turn her down flat, she promised herself that she would make the offer, anyway, at least making the effort to be his friend.

Pat wasn't very sure he'd want to be her friend, either, but she divulged none of the things she was thinking about Cameron to Mac. She knew that Mac and Tony were close, and she wondered just how close they really were, but chose not to ask. She didn't want Mac mentioning anything to Tony, except that she was seeing him at six. She hoped that Tony would realize that she was terminating the path that the relationship with Cameron seemed to be on. She hung up with Mac, knowing that she was finally headed down the right path in the department of love. She loved Tony. She just hoped that he loved her too.

She curled up in bed and pulled the covers around her, pretending that the quilt was Tony's arms around her. She fell off to sleep, dreaming about Tony. She was finally happy. Being in love was great, being loved back by the same person was marvelous, and she thought that she was.

CHAPTER TWENTY ONE

Pat sat in the booth that they usually sat in at The Little Lunch House, drinking a cup of coffee and waiting for Cameron. She was nervous and edgy, wondering what she would say or even how to approach the subject of changing their relationship to that of just friends. She watched anxiously, as the passersby got thicker on the sidewalk in front of the diner and then thinned out again periodically. Cameron was late. It wasn't like him. Finally, at seven sharp, she put money on the table to pay for the coffee and got up to leave.

She said good-bye to all the servers. They were all on a first-name basis now and friends of a sort. She had their envy at being blessed with the affections of Officer Scott, the local hero aimed directly at her heart. She hadn't said anything about her reasons for meeting him that night, as they all swooned over his photograph in the paper.

It was a pretty big deal to the crowd that Sunny had made bail and gotten out, and all the girls had asked her if she knew what Cameron's feelings on that fact had been. She didn't even try to speculate or act as if she were informed. She just said that they hadn't had a chance to discuss it yet.

Pat started toward the door when the squeals of one server called her attention to the door.

"He's here! Oh, there he is! Hi, Cameron," she shrieked as if Elvis Presley had just come back from the dead and walked into the tiny diner to ask for her hand in marriage. She waved with such enthusiasm that Pat was afraid that her hand might fall off if she didn't stop. The rest of the girls joined in smiling, waving, and batting their eyelashes. Pat wanted to get sick, but instead, she just grinned at the silliness of the sight. Cameron would be fine after she ended their relationship. Every girl in town wanted to be in her position—every girl, except her.

She met Cameron at the door. He was still in his police officer's uniform, and his cheeks wore a rosy hue as he waved back. When Pat got a little closer, she put her hand over her nose and mouth. Her eyes watered until she could barely see through the blur of tears. He reeked with the foulest stench that she had ever smelled.

"Ugh, what happened to you?" she asked, forgetting why they were meeting in the first place.

"I had to wrestle a guy that was robbing a fish market. I jumped him during the crime, and we landed in a huge vat of fish. Flounder, I think," he said, pretending to smell himself and know one fish's smell from another's.

The servers all swooned. Their hero had captured another crook. In their eyes, he was the most wonderful man alive, and they would've given anything to be in Pat's shoes. Pat wished with all her heart that she felt the same way about Cameron as they did. She had tried, but that spark just did not occur. She felt bad about having to end the dating part of their relationship, but she was completely head over heels in love with Tony. She knew that now.

"I need to get home to shower and change my clothes," Cameron said, taking her hand and pulling her along behind him. She tried to protest but was unsuccessful, as a motorcycle pack roared by them. She followed him to the squad car involuntarily, which smelled almost as bad as he did, and he drove to his apartment. She opened up her window and hung her head out, trying to live through the short ride, instead of dying from the smell.

She had never been to Cameron's apartment and was thankful that it was only a few miles away from the diner. She followed him inside, thinking that the privacy of the apartment might be a better place to break up, if you could even call what she was doing breaking up with someone. They had only been on a few dates, and he had never even kissed her, not really. Not the way Tony had.

"Make yourself at home," he said, rushing into a room and out of her sight.

She sat on the small, mustard yellow love seat that he was using as a living room sofa and looked around. The apartment was a tiny square cut into four. The walls were eggshell and almost barren, except an anime poster and a picture of him in his police uniform next to Tom. There was one worn-out end table with discolored wood and a lamp that looked as if it had been retrieved from a junkyard.

She could see into the room that acted as a kitchenette. It had a small stove, a microwave, and a toaster. There was a coffeepot, but it was still in the box. The kitchenette, unlike the rest of the apartment, was sparkling clean, except a little dust. Pat assumed that Cameron wasn't much of a cook and had most likely not used the room very much. There was a refrigerator on the opposite wall. Pat could see about five inches of the front of it as she sat. The move-around-ability line in the middle of the kitchenette couldn't have been more than three feet or so. It was a very tight space to cook in. Part of her understood why he didn't bother, considering he was a single man and all. He probably ate out a lot.

Since it was one-eighth of the room, she assumed that the other side was a bathroom. The room Cameron had entered would have had to be the bedroom, and the entrance to the bathroom would have had to be inside.

The smell of lemon wafted through his tiny home, and the sound of the shower running was as clear as a train whistle would have been. She remembered when the officers at the crime scenes had told her to use lemon shampoo to get the smell of death by drowning off her. It was the kind of stench that clung to a person within seconds. She shivered at the memory.

She was very glad that the fish smell had not clung to her in the same manner. She wondered if that was because she had only been exposed to it for a few minutes. A shout from the other room interrupted her train of thought. It was Cameron.

"Babe, could you grab a towel for me? I forgot to bring one in," Cameron's voice shouted above the noise that the running water was making.

Pat went through the same door Cameron had cautiously, rolling her eyes at the dopey nickname he'd chosen this time. She wasn't his "babe" or anybody else's. She didn't want to see anything that she shouldn't and wasn't very sure that the bathroom and bedroom were situated the way she had assumed. What if the door was open, and she could see through the shower stall? Anything was possible.

The door creaked, as she pushed it open. She breathed a sigh of relief when she discovered that her assumption had been correct and that she had indeed entered into his bedroom. The entrance to the bathroom was against the same side of the wall of the apartment that the kitchenette was. The door was slightly ajar, but she couldn't see into the room.

The bedroom had a twin bed that was unmade, a small desk and a chair, and a computer sitting on top of the desk. There were framed newspaper clippings on the wall with headlines about his war hero parents, and that was it as far as decorations went.

"In the closet on the left; no right," he yelled, correcting himself in the process.

She looked at the wall alongside the bathroom door. There were three closets. The closet on the left was long and thin like her mother's linen closet was, so she figured that Cameron meant this closet. She opened it, and it was a shoe rack. The middle closet contained clothes, and the one to the right contained blankets, sheets, towels, and other assorted items and things he had no place for. Pat had a drawer for that type of thing called a junk drawer in her desk. She grabbed a towel, reached into the tiny steam-filled bathroom, and placed it on the sink. It was within reaching distance, and she was grateful not to have to enter the room.

"Thanks, hon," he hollered over the water and through the steam.

Pat wished that he hadn't called her that. He was getting too into the relationship, and it was much too fast by anyone's standards. It was a total turn-off for her. She shook off the thought. It would end quickly enough, she knew. She felt comfort in the knowledge.

She went over to take a closer look at the newspaper clippings hanging on the wall. She read about Carroll John the third and Antoinette, also known as Toni Scott. How odd that his father's name was Carroll, a name usually bestowed on females, and his mother's name was Toni, a name usually bestowed on a male, a male nickname. Why did that suddenly strike a cord in her nerves that felt like sandpaper?

Suddenly, something didn't sit well in her stomach. Something felt oddly out of place. She felt suddenly suspicious. Had he lured her into his bedroom in hopes of being with her in a marital way?

She listened for the water in the shower, and it was still running. She decided to go back to the love seat to wait for

Cameron. She was more determined than ever to end the relationship. She felt so weird about things that she didn't even want him to join them in trying to prove Sunny's innocence.

As she sat down, she noticed a brown paper package sticking out from underneath the love seat. She pulled it out. It was a wrapped box addressed to a company she'd never heard of, general delivery to a post office, in a town unfamiliar to her.

She noticed that there was no return address on the box. That meant that it would go to the post office, and a person from the company that it was addressed to would pick it up. The post office could not return it because there was no one to return it to, and there was no postage on it. Obviously, it would have to be paid for at the other end. That was an odd way to send a package, in her opinion.

She shoved it back where it belonged and thought for a moment. The weird, uncomfortable feeling was overwhelming. Was she just nervous about admitting that she didn't love him? She shook off the feeling, wishing that it was all behind her, and glanced around for a magazine to read or something to keep her busy until he was out of the shower and fully dressed.

The shoe closet had not closed properly, so she went over and tried to close it. Something was in the way, so she opened the door to correct the problem. There was something sticking out at the very bottom of the closet just enough to be the annoying menace that kept the door from closing. It looked like an oblong black box at first, but when she got a little lower and examined it closer, it was not a box at all. It was a black, ankle high boot. The sole of the boot was a platform about six inches high. Upon scrutiny, she discovered that there were two. She shoved them back into the little closet and forced the door shut.

Her mind was reeling. What was it that Mac had said about the guy who had attacked her? She'd thought that he was the Frankenstein monster or something like that. Big feet, wasn't that it? She felt the blood drain from her face.

She stopped and listened to the water. It was still running, so she knew that Cameron did not know that she had found his boots. She decided that if she kept listening to the water, she would know when Cameron was getting out of the shower and the dry-off time would allow her to escape to her position back on the putrid yellow love seat.

She opened the clothes closet and looked for a thick coat or something of that nature. Behind his uniforms, tucked way in the back was a coat. It was more like a large suit jacket. It was black with thick, satin lapels. It was much too large to be Cameron's jacket. The coat felt much too thick to be just a suit jacket, so she moved the hangers to look closer. Underneath the coat was a muscle-man Halloween costume. There were largely exaggerated foam bulges where there would've been muscles on a person like that.

The water was still running, as she tucked the suit and coat back into the place she had found them. Mac had said that the clothes were thick. Her brain was in a swirl of frenzy. There was no question in her mind. Cameron had to be the Baby Diaper Murderer.

She still heard the water running, as she straightened out the hangers to be exactly as she'd found them. She felt fright deep down inside her. She turned to go out of the room, and this time, she was not going to sit down and wait for him. She was going right out the door and not going to stop until she got to Tony and Mac in the public view of the Sound Rave. She had to get away from him without letting him know what she had found.

She turned to go and looked right into Cameron's face. Apparently, there was a door leading to the tiny living room. He'd come around the other way. She felt a surge of fear radiate from her chest to her limbs. Her heart skipped a beat—probably several—and then sped up faster than it ever had in the past.

The water was still running in the background. Daggers shot from his eyes, as he stood in front of her wearing only a towel. It was eerie. It was as if someone different—an entity not of this world—was standing in front of her using Cameron's body as his cover. He looked evil. Satan was most likely the being programming the black heart contained in Cameron's body at that moment. The water spurts were still going strong, and he was holding his nightstick in his hand.

Without so much as a word, he hit her with it, aiming straight for her head. She brought her hand up to block the blow the way she had learned to in karate class. It really hurt, and she cried out. What was it that Sensei said?

He swung again, and she blocked it again, but this time he got her shoulder. She tried to push him away. She might as well have been trying to move the wall. She formed her hand into a palm heel and shot it straight at his nose, trying to aim upward. She missed. It hit his forehead. It didn't even faze him. He hit her again repeatedly.

It hurt, and she screamed at the pain. Panic filled her mind. She couldn't think. She couldn't make it stop. He hit her again in the head hard, and she fell to the floor. For the first time in her relationship with Cameron, she saw stars. That was just before the final blow, which turned her world black on impact.

CHAPTER TWENTY TWO

Mac was looking at her watch, wondering where on earth Pat was. It wasn't like her to be late. Tony brought sodas back to the table for them to drink while they waited. He was also a little more than worried, but he wondered if Mac had just misunderstood the time.

After what had occurred between Pat and him the night before, he was convinced that she would not stand them up. He was sure that her feelings matched his own and that she cared for him too deeply to hurt his feelings by being this late. It was 8 o' clock.

"Where could she be?" He finally stated his mind aloud.

"She said that she was meeting Cameron first. She was going to try to recruit his help." Mac shrugged as she spoke. "Maybe she hasn't convinced him yet," she added.

"Where were they meeting?" Tony asked, getting an uneasy feeling about the situation.

"At The Little Lunch House," Mac answered.

"Then, that's where we're going," Tony said.

He and Mac ran nearly the entire way to the diner. When they got there, the servers told them the smelly fish story, as they swooned again on Cameron's behalf. Tony figured that Pat probably had gone home to change if any of the smell had gotten on her. He and Mac decided to go over to her dorm and meet her there. Tony hoped with all his might that he would not find Cameron there with her. It would kill him if he thought she'd played him for a fool. He was in love with her.

Pat's head hurt, and the room was blurred and spinning when she woke up. She wasn't in Cameron's apartment anymore; she was sure of that. She tried to focus.

She heard water running in the background, and she was lying on a bed. Her hands were tied behind her, and her feet were tied tightly with duct tape. The room rather looked like hers, but it wasn't hers. She was lying on a plastic tarp thrown over the bed. It was uncomfortable and made her sweat. It hurt her skin in some spots on her back, and she realized that she was naked.

She looked around the best she could, which created excruciating pain in her head and neck, but it was worth it. She spotted a picture of Big Ralph and Tiffany-Crystal. She knew that she was in Sunny's room, but why? What had happened to Cameron? Why was she tied up, and where was Sunny? She wanted Sunny to untie her so that she could call the police and tell them what she knew about Cameron. She tried to shout for her but realized that her mouth was also duct taped. She squirmed around, trying to loosen her bonds to no avail. The Frankenstein monster of Mac's drugged memory emerged from the bathroom.

He pulled the stocking off his face. It was Cameron wearing the ridiculous costume and the platform boots. He wore the coat over the suit. He was huge and scary. He easily looked as big as Sunny in them. She made a noise, but he didn't remove the tape. Instead, he decided to talk to her. She was horrifically terrified as he spoke.

"The first girl was the hardest, but it got easier after that. It was the smell that I hadn't expected," he said with a look on his face that seemed as if the story was a happy memory. He let the police in on several murders by phone so that he wouldn't have to deal with that again.

"I had to figure out a way to get you involved. You see, I fell for you right away," he said, sitting down on the bed beside her. She struggled. She wanted him to move away, to let her go. Instead, he stroked her hair, shushed her, and continued.

"I drugged the photographer with Quaaludes I smashed into powder. The downer in the popular seventies drug busts. I gave him just enough to stop him from functioning properly, or at least I tried to. He got a little too much once. I have access to all kinds of things in the evidence room," he continued, still stroking her hair. "I gave all my babies some roofies, the date rape drug of choice by low lives everywhere," he laughed as if the whole thing was a big joke.

"The pièce de résistance was Sunny, though—our big, gay, stupid friend, Sunny. I slipped Spanish fly into her soda while you two were in the bathroom. That drug is legendary. It was supposed to be for us. I hoped you'd be less inhibited; no, not hoped—I knew. Especially when I saw how Sunny reacted to it. Sunny would have humped a goat that night to get sexually satisfied. I gave her a big dose. Yours and mine," he said tauntingly. He acted as if he were proud of himself. Pat felt sick. He had gotten away with all of it.

"It played out beautifully. I was the hero; I got the girl; the big goof was gone forever," he said and shook his head.

She couldn't speak. She couldn't protest or even lie to save herself from him. She listened and tried to reconcile herself to the impending death. She prayed silently for the Lord to forgive any sins she might have committed and to take care of all the people she loved until she could see them again in the kingdom of heaven. Tears rolled down her cheeks, but Cameron didn't care. He just continued telling his story as if it mattered one iota to her if she heard it.

She thought of Tony. How cruel life was to have let her have him, but not experience the love she felt for him to its fullest.

"You just couldn't let it go, could you? Sunny could never let it go, either. You two are alike that way. The teacher told her to do a report. She did it on my parents who were town heroes because of their war history. She dug too deep and found out the truth. I told her I'd kill Tiffany-Crystal if she ever told anyone. The blimp knew I would too. I was bigger than her then," he said, laughing harder.

"This is going to be the first of many crime sprees with me starring as the hero. I am going to do wondrous things of epic proportion with my life. There's only one problem," he said as if he wanted her opinion on something.

"I don't know whether to make you the last victim in Sunny's case or the first victim in the next case. Do you want me to tell you about the next one?" he asked her with pure hatred dripping from his eyes and lingering in his tone of voice.

She couldn't answer, and he knew it, but his mind had clearly snapped. He got up and picked up a large kitchen Ginsu knife. She knew that it wasn't Sunny's knife. He had to have brought it with him.

"I'm going to find young, pure girls like you and deflower them," he said, turning the knife gently back and forth.

"I'm going to cut the proverbial cherry right from the vine. The best part is that I'm going to pin it on your little friend Tony. He is the product of rape. Did you know that? Then, his alcoholic mother abused him. After that, I'm taking down that little kung fu bitch you've been hanging around with," he added, grinning at her.

"But since we're here already, I'll just put the last nail in Sunny's coffin. She'll definitely get the death penalty for this.

I'll be the grieving boyfriend. Think about all the women that will want me," he said excitedly.

He pulled her from the pillow flat onto her back and climbed on her chest with his knees on each side of her head. What was he doing? She struggled and squealed from underneath the tape.

She had never been more frightened than she was at that moment. Terror gripped her brain, and horror ripped through her mind. He ripped the duct tape off her mouth without mercy and held his hand over it, instead.

The stinging pain seared through her jaws. He reached over and took a little cup off Sunny's night table. He put one hand around her neck with his fingers to steady her head using her jaw. There was baby lotion, powder, and something that looked like loose wipes up there too. Reality infiltrated her brain. He was choking her. This was it. She struggled and cried.

The cup had brown liquid in it that smelled as if it was an alcoholic beverage of some sort, as it got closer to her face. She didn't want it and tried once again to free herself. She moved her head back and forth, but it did little to deter the inevitable. She began to sob from deep in the back of her throat. He held her nose. She choked on the liquid. She was petrified. She wanted him to stop.

"Now, take your medicine like a good little girl," he said, removing his hand to rub her throat, forcing her to swallow what was left in her mouth.

She tried to scream, but he poured more liquid into her mouth and held her nose. She tried to move her head back and forth, but his knees held it in place. She swallowed, choked, and coughed until he'd gotten about two and a half ounces into her.

The rest was all over her face, but it didn't matter to him. Bathing her would take care of that mess. The date rape drug was in the alcohol. Reality slipped away from her mind's grasp within seconds, and only minutes passed before she was completely out of it, and Cameron had total control.

He untied her, removed the duct tape, and carried her to the bathtub. He put her into the water gently, slowly submerging her until she was completely underneath the surface. Little bubbles popped to the surface, and he knew that it wouldn't be long before she was dead. It excited him.

CHAPTER TWENTY THREE

Tony and Mac crossed the campus and were beside the fountain when they noticed the lone squad car outside Pat's dorm. Tony felt uneasy but not alarmed. He assumed that he'd been mistaken about the feelings returned to him by Pat. He just hoped that he wasn't going to walk in on a cozy lovers' scene. Mac was a little worried, though. She wondered why Cameron had brought the squad car. Had Sunny done something to warrant his arresting her or taking her into custody again?

They went up to Pat's dorm room and knocked. No one answered, and the door was locked. Tony took his student identification card out of his pocket and slid it between the doorjamb. The lock popped open without any trouble. The lights were off, and Pat wasn't home.

A sense of panic went through Tony. Had they been wrong about Sunny, and was Pat at the mercy of her killing spree at that very moment? He took off at a full run around the corner of the hall and down toward Sunny's room at the far end of the hall with Mac right on his heels. She'd figured out his train of thought without asking him to speak it. She too was engulfed in panic. Quickly, he was far ahead of her.

Tony tried to push the door open. It was locked. He banged on it and then frantically searched his pocket for the credit card that would grant him access. He had dropped it somewhere en route.

"Get out of my way," Mac yelled from down the hall, bolting toward the door with a look of sheer determination on her face. He stepped aside just in time.

She jumped high, pushing one leg out in front of her, turning to the side, and tucking the other one underneath. She stuck her heel out and curled her toes back on an angle. Her hands went into fists up by her face, and she shouted "Kiya" as if she were in a Bruce Lee or Jackie Chan movie.

If Tony hadn't seen it, he would never have believed it. The door crashed to the ground, taking the doorjamb in its entirety with it. She landed on top of it like a cat, on her feet, and yelled, "Bathroom."

Tony got by her, as Cameron came through the bathroom door. Reality overtook him. Tony pushed Cameron to the side and went in to pull Pat from her watery tomb. There were no more little bubbles.

Cameron tried to blast past Mac. He was sure that Pat was dead, and Tony could do nothing but dry her off. He was also sure that he could still pin the murder on Sunny. He didn't realize that he had pulled the stocking off his face, and they knew exactly who he was.

Mac wasn't having anything of the kind. She would not let him escape. She was ready, and this time, she wasn't drugged. She kicked him smack in the face, and he fell backward, right on his butt. Tony pulled Pat's lifeless body from the tub.

"No, oh please, no," he wailed with anguish, as he laid Pat's still body on the tile floor. It distracted Mac long enough for Cameron to grab her legs and take her to the floor. He scrambled to his feet, kicked her in the ribs with the platform shoes, incapacitating her momentarily, and escaped out the door.

Mac dragged herself into the bathroom to see if she could help Tony. They heard the squad car pull away as they did CPR on Pat. Tony was openly crying, as he struggled to save the love of his life. He begged her repeatedly to respond. Mac helped him by trying to get her heart to beat.

Tony pleaded with the Lord, begging Him not to let her die. It would be too cruel. He had never loved anyone like that before. Mac's heart bled for him, as he openly pleaded while they fought hard to save her. Just when Mac thought the end had come, and they would not win the fight, Pat moved. Mac backed off and watched, placing an arm across Tony's chest to stop him.

Suddenly, Pat coughed and sputtered. He quickly turned her on her side, and water came pouring out of her mouth. She was alive. She was drugged badly, but she was alive. Mac ran for the phone to call an ambulance, and then she dialed the police station to tell the true story of what had happened and who the real Baby Diaper Murderer was.

The police officer on the other end of the line listened with incredulous disbelief, but didn't dismiss the story just because the culprit was a fellow police officer. He wrote down everything and put out an all-points bulletin on Cameron Scott. He let all the officers know that Cameron was suspected of murder and that he could be armed and dangerous.

By the time the A.P.B., as the police called the all-points bulletin, was out, the ambulance had arrived to take Pat to the hospital. Tony and Mac rode with her. She was incoherent, and the medics hoped that she hadn't sustained any brain damage. They were not sure what drugs she had been given or how much, and her breath had alcohol residue according to the man reporting in to the hospital they were veering toward. Tony was beside himself with worry. What had that monster done to her?

"Will she be okay?" Mac asked in her innocent little-girl voice. Tony looked up at her. He tended to forget how young she was. Her eyes were so big, and the blue in them had crystallized from crying on behalf of Pat's life. The black lashes were lined with red, and silent tears fell down her cheeks without warning.

"We'll do the best we can," the medic taking her vital signs assured Mac gently. She nodded and watched Pat for any sign of normalcy. There was none.

CHAPTER TWENTY FOUR

Pat woke up. She strained her eyes trying to see. The room around her was nearly pitch-black. Her head hurt, and her eyes blinked, feeling pain from a dim light cast into the room from under the door. She felt cold.

For some reason, she felt frightened. She prayed that no one was with her—like a monster under the bed or one in the closet—especially not the Frankenstein legend come to life. She tried hard to scan the room. Her breath felt labored. It was as if she couldn't take a deep breath. Then, she saw it.

A silhouette lurked in the shadows. There was a sinister silvery glint of metal, as he stepped out of the shadows. He drew closer to her. The silhouette was still a blur. Her heart pounded, and her chest ached as he loomed over her.

It was the monster—the one that paled every nightmare she'd ever had by comparison. Terror filled her mind. She tried to scream, as he thrust the metal object toward her. He wore an evil smile on his face. Terror gripped Pat, as he lunged. She closed her eyes and screamed, as pain seared through her body, infiltrating every nerve ending possible.

"No," she wailed in anguish. "Somebody, help me. Help me, please," she shouted in spasms from the back of her throat, pleading for her life, and begging for mercy, as the assailant repeatedly bludgeoned her with the knife.

"It's okay, I'm not going to let anyone hurt you," a gentle voice said, finding its way through her terror, stroking her hair lovingly. Pat blinked her eyes. The light hurt, but she could see that she was not in her own room. She sobbed uncontrollably, as the gentle, raspy voice instructed someone to press the call button.

"Am I dead?" Pat sobbed. The stranger held Pat in her arms, making gentle shushing sounds, and rocking her. Pat shook while she sobbed. She couldn't control that, either.

"No, you're not dead," the stranger said soothingly. Pat calmed down slowly, as the woman held her. Reality seeped into her brain, and she realized that she was in no eminent danger. It had been a terrible nightmare. She wasn't dead. She was very much alive and in some strange bedroom.

"Who are you?" Pat asked the woman when she could comprehend that she was in a hospital room, and the woman might just be a nurse.

"My name is Cyndi," the woman answered, still holding her.

"Are you a nurse?" Pat asked, confused.

Cyndi was wearing a sequined lime green tank top and a lime green flowing skirt with three sections and sandals. A printed scarf was around her waist that was all different color greens on it, and she wore big silver hoop earrings. She wore several silver bracelets and red lipstick that matched her red nail polish. Her hair was short and very dark and curly. She wasn't dressed as if she were a nurse. If there had been a bandana wrapped around her head, Pat would have thought that she was a gypsy. The thought crossed her mind that she might be hallucinating or something like that, but at least this scene wasn't an unpleasant one.

"No, I'm here visiting my friend's mother in the next bed," she answered. Pat glanced over at the woman in the next bed. She and her daughter were staring at her with wide eyes and curiosity.

"Hi," they said in unison. One was a soprano, and the other was an alto, so they sounded as if they were doing a hello duet. Pat waved and tried to focus.

"Do I know you?" she asked Cyndi.

"No, you don't. I heard you screaming and came over to see if you were all right. You've been thrashing around all week. They said that you were in a coma," Cyndi informed her.

Tony and Mac walked into the room just then. Mac was carrying a bag of assorted fruit and was munching on a peach.

"I'm a real fruit freak," she was informing Tony when they spotted Pat and saw that she was awake.

"Call the doctor," Tony shouted the order and was at her side within seconds.

"My friend pressed the call button about a minute ago. The nurse will be in shortly. They think it's her mother. I don't think that they realize that your friend here is awake," Cyndi said.

"Although her screams could've waked the dead," the woman that Cyndi was visiting said. If she only knew how close to the truth that statement was, she would probably have requested a room change, Mac thought. Tony had a similar thought, but neither voiced it aloud. Pat was still fighting to concentrate on what was going on. It was surreal—like something out of an old movie.

The nurse came in, asking what she could do for Pat's hospital room neighbor, as she came through the door and stopped short when she saw the gathering around Pat's bed and that her eyes were open. She quickly assessed that she was obviously coherent as well, although she had no idea why Cyndi was sitting on the bed holding her instead of Tony, Mac, or her parents. She composed herself quickly.

"How are you feeling, Miss Farmer?" the nurse walked over and asked, as she dutifully pressed Pat's call button.

"What's going on?" A female voice came over the intercom.

"Miss Farmer is awake. Could you find the doctor and send him in? Also, Miss Farmer's parents are in the lounge. Would you wake them and send them in as well?" the nurse asked.

"They've been up for days. I made them lie down," the nurse explained to Pat.

"Right away," the voice on the intercom said. There was no question that the voice was impressed and relieved at the news. Cyndi removed herself gently from the scene and went back to her friend's mother in the next bed when the doctor came in.

The doctor asked everyone to leave for a few minutes while he checked Pat over. He gave her a clean bill of health, except a slight fever. Pat was glad to hear that she was okay. He wanted her to stay in the hospital until the fever was gone, though.

"What happened after he fed me the drugs?" Pat asked Tony and Mac after she finished explaining what had gone on before they got there. She wondered if he had raped her or cut the cherry from the vine, as he'd called it. The thought frightened her, but she was afraid to speak the words.

"He put you in the bathtub and drowned you," Tony answered.

"But was there... did he...?" Pat couldn't get the words out.

"No, he didn't touch any victims in a sexual manner," the nurse said, bringing in the medicine for her fever.

So, Pat had been the supposed last victim of Sunny and not the first of the next murderous spree. The news was welcome.

She accepted it gratefully. She felt as if she'd been run over with a steamroller.

Pat wondered how the nurse knew what she was trying to ask. It didn't really matter, as long as Cameron hadn't hurt her that way. What he had done was bad enough.

"You should have seen Miss Mighty Mac here. She did a flying side kick into the door and literally crashed through it. If I hadn't seen it myself, I would've never believed it. She landed on her feet too, the little shit," Tony gushed, totally impressed, as he remembered the scene vividly.

"If I hadn't seen it myself, I never would have believed it, either," Mac admitted.

"You could've fooled me," Tony assured her in an impressed tone of voice. He put his fists up and weaved his head back and forth slightly in a teasing manner. The three friends laughed. "Then, she kicked him so hard that he landed right on his ass," Tony continued. Pat was impressed. Cameron wasn't a little guy without the suit.

"Yeah, then I saw you lying on the floor. It stopped me cold. You were too still," Mac said, scrunching her face, shaking her head with eyes drawn downward and shivering at the memory that would remain forever etched in her brain. Her facial expression gave away her massive remaining emotional trauma. "And the creep kicked me with those great big clodhoppers again," she added, pulling up her shirt to expose purple and yellow bruising on her ribcage. "I really thought he'd broken my ribs this time," she complained. It looked like it hurt.

"Wow, Mac," Pat said with true awe. It was all she could think of in the moment that no words would ever clearly describe.

"And then I let him get away," Mac admitted.

"You did not," Tony spoke sternly. "You helped me save her life," he said, correcting her and motioning to Pat. They filled her in on the parts of the story that she had not known.

"Did they arrest him outside?" Pat asked, referring to Cameron.

Tony had not wanted to tell her that he'd totally escaped. The police did not know where he'd disappeared to. No one even knew where he was from. According to the FBI, he didn't even exist. He'd never graduated from any law enforcement academy, either. They didn't have a clue how he'd gotten a job on the force. All his credentials, though masterfully created, were fakes.

Pat gasped. He really had followed in his parents' footsteps if the story that Mac had found out about them from Sempai was true. Somehow, she knew that it was.

"I know where he is," Pat said with a light bulb going off in her brain.

"Where do you think he is? Did he tell you before he tried to kill you?" Mac and Tony asked at the same time as Cyndi did from behind the curtain. Tony pulled the curtain open, and Cyndi shrugged and grinned.

"We're in very close quarters here," she said, and there was no doubt in anyone's mind that Cyndi had figured out who Pat was.

"I think that he might have just gone home," Pat answered, bringing everyone back to the more important situation at hand.

"Where is home?" Tony asked, confused. He hadn't gone back to his apartment. The police had staked it out and gone through it with a fine-tooth comb. They'd found nothing. He'd taken everything. What did Pat mean?

"His home is in the same town as Sunny's. He lives on the outskirts. They went to the same school, for heaven's sake," Pat said forcefully.

"No one could be that stupid," Mac said pointedly.

"Tell the police, anyway," Cyndi interjected her opinion. They all agreed, and Mac went off to call the police and give them the new information. She knew that they'd be coming to the hospital to question Pat, anyway. Cameron's partner Tom had said so. He'd also apologized profusely for not knowing what Cameron was doing. He, too, felt like a fool. As far as Mac was concerned, he should get in line. Cameron had duped them all.

CHAPTER TWENTY FIVE

A week went by before the police caught up to Cameron. He had indeed gone home but only to get some things and flee from the law from there. Mr. and Mrs. Scott were arrested on the spot, as they were caught off guard. It seemed that they had disappeared into a country where they were allowed diplomatic immunity to escape prosecution for treason in America. At some point, they snuck back in undetected by anyone and were living happily ever after as war heroes in the small town. Cameron had not informed them about the mess he'd gotten himself into. Instead, he cleaned out their bank accounts and left them behind to rot in his wake.

Cameron was found sleeping on a park bench four towns away with a bottle of rum half gone in one hand and a bottle of pills that he had been too cowardly to swallow all of in the other. He was passed out and drunk. His fake identification and wallet were in his pockets.

When they hauled him into the station there, he was still stinking drunk and reeked of alcohol mixed with severe body odor. He looked as if he was trying to live undercover among the homeless until the heat died down, the police officers had told Tom. The unofficial gossip was that he'd lost his mind— was criminally insane and schizophrenic. Some believed that he was faking, but the criminal psychologist at the precinct that found him said he was not.

Pat believed that he had lost his mind as well when she heard about it. The look in his eyes just before he bludgeoned her with his nightstick remained steadfast in her memory. Still, she found it odd that he would go through all that and not have a back-up plan. He had used false identification, had an extensive knowledge of drugs, had weaseled his way on to the police force, and had formed the Baby Diaper Murder plans all on his own with only an agenda.

He had no accomplices, not even his parents. If he had used his mind for real law enforcement, she had no doubt that he would've gone far. Instead, he lost his mind, which had to have been a brilliant one.

Pat was relieved to hear that he had been captured on the day she was released from the hospital. She decided that she would put more of her self into learning self-defense. It was obviously a useful thing to know. She donned her Gi and drove over to the school.

As she walked across the parking lot, a feeling of anxiety overwhelmed her. She was afraid again. She was about to turn around and forget the whole thing when a guy on a yellow motorcycle whizzed past her. It was a nice bike. She had always had a fascination with motorcycles but had never ridden on one. She watched it pull into a parking space in front of the school. The motor whirred down, and the rider began to disembark.

A tall, slender figure dressed in black leather and a black helmet got off the bike. The scene mesmerized Pat, as the unknown biker took off his helmet. She was shocked when the mystery man turned out to be Sensei. She thought about bolting for her car, but it was too late. He spotted her right away.

"Pat, it's nice to see you back," he said, walking over to her with the helmet tucked under his arm. "I heard what happened," he continued, as they walked together toward the school.

"Yes, I wondered if my program was still in effect because the month is over with," she lied. She hoped that it wasn't and that he would send her home. He assured her that the month would start from that very minute and that he would see to it personally. She smiled. He really was a nice man.

She felt comfortable with him and became a little more at ease, as she expressed her new set of fears to him. He was kind and gentle but firm in his opinion that she should train now in karate for all that she was worth. It couldn't have been a more profound time in her life to take that step, he'd said with a gentle force exuding from his words. Part of Pat agreed; in fact, most of her did. She was just so frightened of everything now. It was an aftereffect of nearly being murdered, she guessed.

He put his arm around her in a fatherly fashion. Somehow, without words, he assured her that everything was going to be all right—that all she had to do was do it, and the rest would fall into place.

Sempai jumped up from behind the reception desk and made her way through the crowd, pulling Pat right into her arms as she and Sensei entered the school. Pat let her until the shaking stopped.

"We were so worried about you. Welcome back," she said, extending her arms out just far enough to search Pat's eyes.

Pat felt her searching. It was as if Sempai were her mother incarnate. That was exactly the way her mother had reacted when she woke up. Sempai seemed to find what she was looking for, and Pat seemed to pull some strength from her in a kind of bizarre osmosis type of mind exchange without using words.

It was wonderfully strange. She felt loved and wanted here. No one was holding anything back. Reserved was a word people used in the outside world; here, they just let everything flow. Pat liked it, and she was grateful for it.

Mac was standing at the door of the mat with Betsy, and they both urged her on. Joshu came out of the back and threw his arms around her too. She finally made her way to the locker room and then headed for the mat to train.

Mac stopped her for a turn at hugging her too. Pat held her tightly, knowing that if it had not been for her, she would probably be dead. Knowing that mortality existed was one thing, but staring it in the face and knowing it existed was yet another thing altogether.

"I have a favor to ask of you," Mac whispered in her ear.

"Anything," Pat said, and she meant it.

My sister is studying criminal psychology, and she'd love to interview you. It would really help her get an 'A.' Will you talk to her?" she asked. Pat nodded.

"I'll do better than that. I kept a journal. I'll print up a copy and give it to her if you want," she answered sincerely.

"Gees, you kept a journal? Did you write everything? Did you write about the end of everything? Did you get the kick in there? It was called a flying side kick, you know... Am I in it?" Mac asked, reacting like the sixteen-year-old girl inside that mature façade and seeming surprised as well. Pat nodded. She chuckled slightly and then realized how much time had gone by since she had spontaneously done that.

"Of course, you are. I'll give you a copy, too, if you'd like," Pat answered.

"That would be awesome, thanks," Mac gushed.

She knew that the whole thing had been as difficult, if not more so, for Pat than it had for Tony and her. Reporters were begging for interviews. Pat had given them but felt awkward about the whole thing. It was going to be an honor to be privy to the journal she had kept from the beginning of the whole saga. She knew at that moment that she was destined to be friends with Pat for a long time. The bond of trust was so thick that it couldn't be broken. They didn't say the words, but they both felt it. They would be friends for life.

They went into class together. Pat knew in her mind that she would edit the journal before giving copies of it to the Mac sisters. She was glad to help someone shooting for a good grade. She had been trying to do the same thing herself when everything got out of control on her. They lined up on the mat in the positions of rank, and class began.

It seemed as if Sensei paid a lot of attention to her that night, not that he hadn't every time she'd trained, but this time, he seemed more determined than ever to get her into mode. He didn't want her to feel frightened ever again; she could tell by his actions.

On Pat's way out of the locker room, she noticed Phil behind the reception desk. He was looking at *The Observationist News* with a parent. There was a picture of Cameron lying in a vat of fish at the fish market. She just assumed that it was the story about the burglary that had occurred on the day that he'd tried to kill her. She felt anger well up within her. How dare they depict that monster in a good light of any kind? As she got closer, the anger dissipated into stifled laughter.

"Look at this," Phil said triumphantly, as he held the paper up so that she could see the headline to the story. It read "Hero Cop Flounders," and the story was less than flattering for the wayward cop.

Cameron had not foiled a burglary in process. He had tripped and fallen into a vat filled with tuna waiting to be filleted. That jerk lied about everything. It served him right that the paper saw fit to print the story, especially given his new "not a hero" status.

"I'll bet that news just made your night," Phil remarked.

Pat grinned widely, but did not answer. Actions spoke a thousand words. It hadn't made her night, but it certainly hadn't hurt it any. The night was made from the second her karate family welcomed her home. That was how she felt all the way to her core about them.

After class was over, she went back to her dorm, feeling new and somewhat revitalized. The end of the semester was just two days away. She needed to do her paper for psychology, and she hadn't even written the first word of it.

She wanted to keep the promise she made to Mac and give her sister and her a copy of the journal. She sat at her journal and stared at it. An idea snapped to attention in her mind. She began editing the journal, but not changing it or leaving anything out, except her innermost feelings for Tony. After that was finished, she wrote a small introduction.

> *Homeostasis can be developed in a healthy manner throughout a child's entire existence, and yet it can change into an unhealthy state of mind easily. It is a matter of human interpretation and the reaction they have to events that occur in their lives.*
>
> *In this journal, I have learned about many different types of homeostatic behavior, my own included. Locked within these pages are secrets to the human mind that I cannot even fathom how to go about unraveling. I name this thesis "Homeostasis: The Human Factor."*

She made a cover for it and prepared it for the professor's approval. The only thing that it was missing was the conclusion. She knew what she wanted to say but was unsure of how to word it. She decided to sleep on it, sure that the words would come if she rested.

What she had experienced, no one could find in a book or see on some television show and completely understand to its fullest potential. She gave herself a mental pat on the back for the brainstorm she believed would elicit the elusive "A" she wanted and crawled into bed for the night.

Just as she curled up under the covers, a knock came to the door. She was nervous, and her heart raced at the fright she was feeling.

"Who is it?" she called out, reaching for the phone and getting ready to dial the three-digit emergency number used in the state to contact the police—9–1–1.

"It's Tony," the muffled voice behind the door said.

She recognized his voice and breathed in a deep sigh of relief. She quickly ran her fingers through her hair and smoothed her bedclothes to look a little more presentable before she opened the door.

Tony stood outside in the hallway with his eyes twinkling and his lips turning that wet red color she had grown to adore. Her body began its inner dance.

"May I come in?" he asked and then walked in before she could answer.

"Sure, come on in," she said sarcastically, teasing him. He laughed through an exhale. He was already sitting on the bed. "You scared me. I was going to call the police," she said seriously.

"I'm surprised that you still trust the police," he said.

"One bad apple doesn't spoil the entire bunch, as they say. Besides, he wasn't really even a police officer," she answered, referring to Cameron.

"We need to talk," Tony said, changing modes. We need to kiss. You need to hold me; I want you, Pat thought, but did not say the words aloud. Her body was going crazy in all directions, and she let it this time. She loved him.

He began describing the relationship between his mother and his biological father. She sat next to him on the bed and faced him so that he could see that he had her undivided attention. Pat squashed her reactions to him so that she could listen. He needed to tell her. It couldn't have been easy for him to decide to do that.

She held his hand while he spoke. Tony was yet another homeostatic pattern forming from an unhealthy background. Apparently, the human factor led him to interpret right from wrong and then choose the right path. It could go either way. The human mind was so complex. She made a mental note to add that fact into the paper as her conclusion to the whole thing as well as the fact that the pattern was forever ongoing and forever forming.

Pat looked into the eyes of the man she loved and loved him more afterward, if that was possible. They lay together in her small bed, entangled in each other's arms, fully clothed, and trusting one another. She listened to Tony breathing lightly as he slept.

The human factor included love, too, she thought—being loved, feeling love, and the ability to give love in return... to see others as the Lord sees them. She smiled to herself, as she snuggled a little closer to him. Perhaps that was what she would do her next psychology paper on. She certainly wouldn't ever again dismiss the importance of psychology. Coupled with forensic pathology and science, it would be hard for a perpetrator to walk away undetected. She even thought that she might make it her minor.

CHAPTER TWENTY SIX

Although things were normal, the semester had ended, and Pat needed to go home for a few weeks to get herself together. She was going to take summer classes, and that meant that there wasn't much time for rest.

She wanted to drop by Sunny's house on her way home and see how she was doing. Candy and Annie piled into the Buick, but the trip was long and quiet. As odd as it was that no one spoke, Pat understood and was thankful for the peace and quiet. That semester at college had changed them all. It had changed everyone. It was as if they shared some kind of special bond in some way. Everyone on campus felt it; so many of the students had talked to her about it.

She dropped Candy and Annie off, thinking that they looked no worse for wear but that they had grown as people in the last few months. They seemed less involved in trivial baloney than they had when she first met them. Neither girl wore a lick of make-up, which for Annie was nothing short of a miracle, and both girls wore sweatshirts and jeans with their hair in ponytails—not very neat ones at that.

Pat waved good-bye and drove towards Sunny's house. She wondered what she might find there. She hoped that Sunny was doing well.

She pulled up in the driveway of the little fairytale house, got out of her car, and knocked on the door.

"Come in," the grunt of Ralph Chyna said, bidding her entrance without ceremony into his home, just as he had all the times before.

Pat opened the door and peeked inside. The scene was the same in some ways but different too. Ralph and his vile friend were positioned in their usual spots, but Ralph did not have a stogie hanging out of his mouth. Tiffany-Crystal had strictly forbidden it, and she was not kidding. She was not serving the men treats of any sort, but was carrying a big basket of diapers in need of washing and telling Ralph to help her carry it before she dumped the basket on his head.

"Sunny, your friend is here," Tiffany-Crystal called, as she deposited the nasty smelling basket on Ralph's lap. She was not singing, but rather, she sounded tired and frazzled. Sunny came out of her room with a spit cloth over her shoulder, and her little brother cradled in her arms.

"Pat," she gushed, as her eyes lit up when seeing the person she considered her best friend. Tiffany-Crystal was barking orders at Ralph by that point. "Come into my room. We'll have peace and quiet in there," Sunny said, and then cooed at the baby.

"What the heck happened?" Pat asked, referring to the change in Tiffany-Crystal.

"Change of life baby, Mom's a bitch," Sunny said, making a wry face and nodding.

Pat laughed right out loud. Sunny grinned. It was about time.

"You look amazing," she said to Sunny.

Sunny must have lost about one hundred pounds. She was still tall, but her figure was actually a figure and a lovely one like her mother's, and she seemed healthier, not to mention that she was smiling.

"Thanks. I have no time to eat. This little guy keeps us all hopping," Sunny replied.

She and Pat talked for a long time, and Pat offered to pick her up in the fall so that they could drive to college together. Sunny was thrilled with that.

Pat confided in Sunny about Tony and her feelings whenever he came near her. When she said that she was in love with him, Sunny was thrilled for her. She knew better than anyone did how lonely being unloved could be.

She told Pat that she had found love too. Her little brother loved her unconditionally. Every time she came into the room, he wanted her. He smiled at her and cooed at her, and he was the most wonderful thing that had ever happened to her.

Pat was so happy for her and glad to hear that Sunny had gone the way of love rather than hate for the little person who had no fault at all in the way she had been treated throughout her lifetime.

Pat drove home feeling better than she had in a long time. She couldn't wait to tell her mother about her feelings for Tony. Her mother already worshiped the ground Tony walked on because he had saved her life. Though he wasn't what she knows her mother would've expected for her in the love department, she was sure that both her parents would be fine with it. His saving her would get him in the door, his inner being would do the rest, of that she was very sure.

She pulled the Buick into her driveway a different person that day. She knew that life had to be lived to the fullest, not taken for granted, and not lived to please anyone other than herself. She had to be true to her own feelings. Life was too easily gone in an instant. For that lesson in homeostasis, she would be forever grateful.

Far away, a man bent down and handed a homeless person a five-dollar bill. The homeless man looked at him, surprised and confused. The Good Samaritan smiled at him in a concerned way.

"Thanks, mister," the homeless man said in a rough, strained voice. He hadn't eaten in a while, and now, he could get some bread at the marketplace.

"Have you seen another man in the same predicament that you are, friend? One who looks like me? I'm looking for someone," the stranger asked. The homeless man shaded his eyes and looked at his angel of mercy a little bit closer.

"You kind of look like Harry. He's a little older, but he looks enough like you that he could be your brother," the homeless man answered and then coughed in a wheezing way. The kind stranger nodded, patted the homeless man on the shoulder, thanked him, and continued on his way.

The stranger entered the post office in the tiny town square, tucked way back in the mountainous farm country. There was a general delivery package waiting for pick-up inside, and he gladly paid the handling costs as the company's representative.

The pretty, young clerk flashed a flirtatious smile at him and asked him his name. The older clerk next to her remembered her youth, as she studied the handsome young man who was saying that his name was Patrick Farmer.

"My friends call me Pat," he added with a magnificent smile. In her silent opinion, the name fit him. Patrick Farmer was a country name. He was so wholesome that he reminded her of freshly baked bread. He was going to stir things up good for this tired old town.

About the Author

Connie Murray Slocum has written many articles on martial arts and has also appeared in *Women's Sports and Fitness* magazine. She contributes to the *TSK Times* newsletter and is known throughout the East Coast of the USA as Tiger Schulmann's MMA school for her writing. Bergen County Justice Center currently employs her and she attends Bergen Community College.

Connie holds a first degree black belt in two different karate styles. She has been on television shows such as "Good Day New York" with a group of fellow students, and on the "Channel 12 News" wtih hostess Melinda Murphy to demonstrate close range defense techniques and wood breaking during a rape awareness segment. She was honored to become part of the Oprah Winfrey "I Love You" special in 1996 in tribute to a young man she wrote a letter about. Connie taught karate to children three to five years old as a volunteer, and she says that this part of her life is one of the most rewarding things she has ever done. Self defense is important to her.

Not knowing her biological father, Connie was raised in an abusive relationship between her mother and the man her mother loved. Connie is one of seven siblings. The family lived for ten years under the tyranny of this man. Sadly, she left home to marry and became a young battered wife. She divorced and remained single until she met the love of her life, David. She and David had three children: a son, James Murray; a daugther who died shortly after birth, Janie-Lynn; and a stillborn son, Jeremy Matthew.

Determined to succeed, Connie forged ahead into the unknown, holding her tiny family together through love and keeping faith in God. She is recently celebrated her twenty-fifth wedding anniversary.

As a woman with strong morals and values, Connie is fun loving and mischevious, with a good sense of humour. Evoking different emotions from people through writing is her fondest dream.

Did you like this book?

If you enjoyed this book, you will find more interesting books at
www.CrystalDreamsPublishing.com

Please take the time to let us know how you liked this book. Even short reviews of 2-3 sentences can be helpful and may be used in our marketing materials.

If you take the time to post a review for this book on Amazon.com, let us know when the review is posted and you will receive a free audiobook or ebook from our catalog. Simply email the link to the review once it is live on Amazon.com, your name, and your mailing address -- send the email to orders@mmpubs.com with the subject line "Book Review Posted on Amazon."

If you have questions about this book, our customer loyalty program, or our review rewards program, please contact us at info@mmpubs.com.

cdp
CRYSTAL DREAMS
publishing

a division of Multi-Media Publications Inc.

Terror in Manhattan

By Ross L. Barber

Jayne Keener is a young, single all-American girl who, like so many newcomers to the world of Cyberspace, finds herself drawn into the shadowy world of cybersex and adult chat rooms. Following the murder of a suave, mysterious Englishman she has met in a Manhattan bar, Jayne finds herself sucked ever deeper into the subculture of Internet chat rooms.

It is in one such room that she encounters Phillip H. Dreedle; professional hacker, convicted rapist and stalker. Suddenly, Jayne's once sane life is turned on its head, and not even her closest friends are what they seem.

ISBN-13:   9781591460404

Available from Amazon.com or your nearest book retailer. Or, order direct at www.CrystalDreamsPublishing.com

Monkey Pudding: A Vietnam Hero's Story

By J.B. Pozner

Lieutenant Steve Simmons returned home from the Vietnam war to find his wife Jennifer in bed with another man. In an enraged scuffle, Jennifer falls down the stairs to her death. After psychiatric treatment in a VA hospital, Steve relocates in a new state with a new career and tries to put his life back together.

Then he meets Christina, heir to an international manufacturing corporation. Uncovering a plot on her life, Steve hires a detective and sets out to find the conspirators.

The story begins with gritty combat scenes in the jungles of Vietnam. The battles continue back home as Steve's post-war traumas are intensified by one bizarre twist after another. The fast pace continues to the dramatic conclusion where Steve may at last taste victory.

ISBN-13:   9781591460077

Available from Amazon.com or your nearest book retailer. Or, order direct at www.CrystalDreamsPublishing.com